THE
RESCUE OF VINCENT

Bob Doerr

Book 2
The Enchanted Coin Series

Mouse Gate Press
1103 Middlecreek
Friendswood, Texas 77546
281-992-3131   281-482-5390 Fax
www.mousegate.com

Library of Congress Control Number: 2014943289

Printed in the United States of America with simultaneous printings in Australia, Canada, and United Kingdom.

FIRST EDITION
1   2   3   4   5   6   7   8   9   10

To all the young readers who have discovered the world of literature and the joy of immersing yourself into the world of fantasy and adventure.

Author: Bob Doerr

 grew up in a military family, graduated from the Air Force Academy, and had a career of his own in the Air Force. Bob specialized in criminal investigations and counter-intelligence gaining significant insight to the worlds of crime, espionage and terrorism. His work brought him into close coordination with the security agencies of many different countries and filled his mind with the fascinating plots and characters found in his books today. His education credits include a Masters in International Relations from Creighton University. A full time author, he has published five mystery/thrillers and was selected by the Military Writers Society of America as its Author of the Year for 2013. The Eric Hoffer Awards awarded No One Else to Kill it first runner up to the grand prize in the category of commercial fiction for 2013. Two of his other books were selected as finalists for the Eric Hoffer Award in earlier contests. Loose Ends Kill was awarded the 2011 Silver medal for Fiction/mystery by the Military Writers Society of America. Another Colorado Kill received the same Silver medal in 2012 and the silver medal for general fiction at the Branson Stars and Flags national book contest in 2012. A novella titled The Enchanted Coin which he wrote with his granddaughter for middle grade readers was released in September 2013. In January 2014, Paragraphs: Mysteries of the Golden Booby, a book Bob co-authored with three other authors, was released. Bob lives in Garden Ridge, Texas, with Leigh, his wife of 40 years, and Cinco, their ornery cat.

Acknowledgement

"I would like to thank Kaiden Kirby in helping me take this book from concept to reality. I also want to thank Emily Smolen and her fifth grade class for providing the special feedback that meant so much to me this past year."

The Book

The Rescue of Vincent: Book 2 in The Enchanted Coin Series is a 36,000 word fantasy adventure targeted at Middle Grade readers. This book is "G" rated.

Imagine being a fourteen year old again and finding a coin that seems to give off a light of its own. The coin has your name on it, and instructs you to toss it into a fountain next to the Tree of Life. That's what happens in *The Rescue of Vincent*, and what starts my protagonist off on a magical adventure that many young boys and girls would love to have.

Characters

Ricky Street: teenage Earth boy and main character who finds the magical coin

Lexus: a teenage girl from the planet Shantell who could be an earthling except for her blue skin

Bebo Thill: a teenage boy from the planet Criax where the people rarely grow to four feet tall and possess no body hair

Vincent Wollitzer: a teenage boy from the strange world where Ricky, Lexus, and Bebo now find themselves. The world council selected Vincent to be the next ruler of their world, but his disappearance now threatens world peace.

Introduction

Would you believe in the magic of a coin you discover that has your name inscribed on it? The coin claims to be magical and even has instructions for you to follow. Would you follow them? What if you did? Would you expect anything to happen? That's what happened to Ricky Street. He found the coin and followed its instructions. What happened to him was totally unexpected and quite frightening. It led him to an adventure that many might think impossible to believe, but it did.

You be the judge.

CHAPTER 1

The wind howled through the Everglades as it whipped up white caps in the larger lakes. Trees and bushes bent under the force of the gale. Leaves and other small debris blew through the air.

A rumble of distant thunder reinforced what Ricky already realized. His coming out here to his favorite fishing spot had been a mistake. Before leaving for work, his mother told him to stay home today. The arrival of the tropical storm had been predicted for days, and the outer bands of the storm had already reached the coast, about forty miles east of Ricky's home.

Ricky knew this, but he figured since the storm had not evolved into a hurricane then it couldn't be that bad. He also knew that his mom always became overly protective when his dad was away on one of his frequent business trips. This time he realized that he should have listened to her.

He decided to reel in his line and head home. The fish weren't biting today anyway. The sky to the east had taken on an ominous darkness, and the breaks in the clouds that had allowed him to see the sky when he arrived at the lake a half hour earlier had shrunk to a handful of narrow streaks out west. He could walk home in fifteen minutes, and if he ran he could get there in half that time.

He hoped that he didn't have to run. In fact, it would be risky to run the first hundred yards between him and the dirt road that he could then follow all the way to his house. To get to the dirt road, Ricky had to cross a field of grasses and weeds that averaged about six inches in height and avoid patches of nasty thorn bushes. What made the area really dangerous, though, were the snakes and alligators that Ricky had occasionally seen in the field.

If he remained alert, he could see any snakes and alligators and stay clear of them. His parents, like parents of all the boys and girls who grew up in the Everglades, taught him about the dangers posed by these reptiles and the need to stay away from them. Sprinting through the field would increase the possibility he'd run into one of them before he saw it, and that could be a deadly mistake.

Ricky hiked up the gentle slope of the field and reached the road without seeing anything other than birds. The dirt road connected a handful of farms to the state road. His grandparents used to farm the land around the house where he now lived with his parents. When his grandfather had an accident about twenty years ago, he had to stop farming. His medical bills piled up, and about the time Ricky was born, his grandparents sold off most of the farm.

A few years later his grandmother became ill, and Ricky's parents decided to move in with his grandparents to help out. Ricky lived in New York until he was three, but he couldn't remember living anywhere else but here. He missed his grandparents, who both passed away within months of each other when he was eight. They took good care of him when his parents were both at work. For a couple of years, his parents hired a woman to watch him, but for the last four years Ricky took care of himself while his mother and father were at work. During the school year he didn't mind the arrangement at all.

Summertime, however, could get a bit lonely. He had Boy Scouts, which he enjoyed, and he played on a Little League baseball team, but he got bored on the days when he had no activities. He wondered if any other kids wished school would hurry up and start.

He saw lighting off in the distance and started jogging. After a few hundred yards, he slowed down and resumed walking. The lightning appeared to be miles away, and the rain hadn't started. He saw his house off in the distance and thought he would beat the rain even if he walked. Besides, Morton's Creek crossed under the road about ten yards ahead, and Ricky enjoyed standing on the small bridge and tossing a stone down at a frog or turtle. His Grandpa had taught him this long ago. You only got one toss with one small stone, and if you hit your target, then fortune would smile on you for the remainder of the day. The small stones they used weren't much bigger than pebbles and never hurt the frogs or turtles.

Ricky picked up a small stone near the edge of the road. Once on the bridge, he looked down at the shallow creek and found the perfect target. A large turtle sat at the water's edge only about twenty feet from Ricky.

"How can I miss?" Ricky asked out loud while he tossed the stone in the air at the turtle.

Just as the stone approached the turtle a bolt of lightning struck an old, dead oak tree about fifty yards behind Ricky. The loud crack of the lightning striking the tree and the corresponding thunder shook the ground around him. Ricky reacted by scrambling off the bridge away from the tree and down to the edge of the creek.

He crouched down and covered his ears with his hands, expecting another lightning strike or loud thunder, but nothing more happened. He slowly stood up and looked over the bridge at the tree. He saw smoke rising from the tree and a small red flame licking at the top of the dead trunk. He slumped back down in relief and saw the turtle.

The turtle stared back at him, half in and half out of the creek.

"Did I get you?" Ricky asked referring to the stone.

The turtle didn't answer, but he did slide the rest of the way into the water and swam away. As it moved off, Ricky noticed something shiny in the water where the turtle had been. He reached in and picked up the item. It appeared to be a coin. For an instant he felt dizzy and imagined that the coin stuck itself to the palm of his right hand.

Ricky stood up and backed away a few steps from the creek. A couple large drops of rain hit him in the face and brought him out of his daze. He still had a third of a mile to go to his home, and it looked like the rain would start pouring any second. Another large drop hit the top of his head.

He put the coin in a pocket and started running home. He entered the front door just as the heavy rain began.

He leaned his fishing pole against the wall by the door. He took off his tennis shoes and placed them on the floor next to the door. If he tracked mud through the house, he knew his mother would make him clean it up. After cleaning the floor a couple of times, he had no trouble remembering to take off his shoes if there was a possibility they contained any mud at all.

"Hey Bucky," he said to the family's pet cat who had come out to greet him. Ricky stroked the white fur on the cat's back. A small patch of grey fur on Bucky's front right leg prevented the cat from being totally white. Bucky purred and rubbed against Ricky's ankles.

After pausing for a moment with the cat, Ricky continued into the bathroom where he tossed his shirt into the laundry basket and dried his head and arms with a towel. He reached into the pocket of his jeans and felt the coin. For reasons he didn't understand, part of his mind told him not to look at the coin. Despite this concern, Ricky took the coin out and looked at it.

Ricky, throw the coin into the fountain in front of the Tree of Life!

The reverse of the coin also had a strange inscription on it: Magic Coin 12 of 51

CHAPTER 2

"Ricky, I'm home!" Shelley Street called as she entered the house through the side door.

"Hey Mom," Ricky answered from his bedroom.

A moment later the door to his bedroom opened, and his mother peeked in.

"How was your day? How much rain did we get?" she asked.

"I haven't checked the rain gauge, but it poured for a couple of hours."

"I'm surprised you haven't checked. Don't you track the rainfall anymore?"

"Yes, but Mom, something weird happened today."

A serious look came across Mrs. Street's face. "What happened?"

Ricky looked at his mother. He began to say something but didn't. He debated with himself whether to tell his mother about the coin or not. Suddenly, Ricky felt like he had no ability to control his decision.

"What son?" She sat down on the bed next to him.

"I found this." The words shot out of his mouth and surprised him. He held up his palm and showed her the coin.

"Oh, isn't that a pretty coin. It really reflects the light, doesn't it? It's not actually round either."

"It's an octagon. It has a message on it," Ricky said.

"Let me see," his mother said.

He gave her the coin, and she studied it.

"I can see it says something, but without my glasses I can't make it out. What does it say?"

"It's a magic coin," he said.

"Why do you say that?"

"The coin says it's a magic coin."

"Then I guess it is," his mother smiled.

Ricky could tell his mother wasn't taking the coin as seriously as he did, but why would she? He still had a hard time believing that the coin was anything more than something he might find at a magic store.

"The coin says to toss it into the fountain in front of the Tree of Life."

"You mean the one at Disney World?"

"I guess so," Ricky said.

"You want to do it?" his mother asked with some enthusiasm. She knew Ricky didn't have much to do during the summer, and the idea of taking Ricky to Disney World appealed to her. "Aunt Jenny would love to see you again."

"That's what I was thinking. I know she likes to see you, too, Mom."

"We haven't been up there in nearly a year, and it's so close. We should go. Jenny can get us in for free, too."

"When can we go?" Ricky asked.

"Let's go this Saturday."

"Will Dad be back?"

"No, not until Tuesday. His route is a long one. Today he's in Detroit, and tomorrow he leaves for Denver, but we can still go. I'll call Jenny. Maybe we can spend Saturday at her apartment."

"That will be fun. Too bad Dad can't be there."

"Well, I better get dinner started. Are you up for macaroni tonight?"

"Sure," Ricky said.

Once his mother left the room, Ricky pulled the magnifying glass out from under his pillow and started analyzing the coin. He didn't know why he hadn't offered the magnifying glass to his mother. Something inside him had told him that it would be better if his mother didn't actually read the inscription. On one side of the coin he could read the words "Magic Coin number 12 of 51." On the other side, the inscription said "Ricky Street - throw the coin into the fountain in front of the Tree of Life."

The coin actually had his name on it. At first he thought that it might be a coincidence, but he now felt that the coin and the message were meant for him. He couldn't explain it, but he felt like he had to follow the instructions.

The next morning, Friday, he took the coin out of his nightstand and looked at it.

"What?" he said out loud. The inscription appeared to have faded to the point that he could barely see it. He grabbed the magnifying glass and looked at the coin. The words were still there, but they had definitely started to fade away.

He took the coin over to the small desk he had in his room, found a piece of paper and a pencil, and wrote the instructions on the paper. He knew he could remember it, but for some reason he felt compelled to make a copy of the message. Better safe than sorry, he thought. What if the trip Saturday got canceled, and he didn't get to go to Disney World for long time? If the inscription disappeared in a few days, a year from now he might doubt that the coin ever said anything. He folded up the piece of paper and put it in his wallet.

As it turned out, Ricky's concern about a delay wasn't necessary. He and his mother drove to Orlando and into Disney World on Saturday morning. They found their passes to the park at the main entrance along with a note from his Aunt Jenny requesting they meet for lunch.

Ricky loved coming to Disney World. He knew it was hard for his mom and dad to get away and bring him here, but in two years he would get his own driver's license. Maybe then he could come up here more often. Maybe he could even get a summer job here and live with his aunt. At lunch he would ask his aunt how hard it was to get a job here.

"Well, Ricky, do you want to go to the Tree of Life first or go on a ride or two?" his mother asked.

"Let's go to the Tree of Life first. That should only take a second, and we can do a ride afterwards."

"Okay."

"Where does Aunt Jenny want to have lunch?"

"She said it was our choice. We'll call her at noon and decide," his mother said.

They talked some more, but Ricky's attention had already turned to thoughts about what might happen when he tossed the coin into the fountain. He didn't expect anything to happen, but as they approached the Tree of Life his imagination started to race with ideas.

"Here we are, Ricky. I don't see any fountain."

They looked around.

"Maybe it's over there," Ricky suggested pointing off to the side.

They walked around to the area Ricky indicated. It looked fairly unkempt, and a couple wheelbarrows and some garden tools were hidden behind some bushes.

"There, Mom, look!"

"That looks a little dumpy. You sure it's the right fountain?"

"Has to be," Ricky said.

"Okay then, toss the coin in, and we'll see what happens. Even I'm getting a little excited."

Ricky and his mother approached the side of the small fountain. Water barely shot out of a small spigot in the middle of the fountain that was not much bigger than a large bird bath. The concrete structure sat on the ground. Ricky looked at the fountain and spotted a fat frog submerged about an inch under the water by the edge.

"That's an easy target," he said, and without any hesitation he tossed the coin gently at the frog. It splashed into the water right on top of the frog.

As Ricky watched the coin start to sink, a bright light flashed in front of him, and suddenly everything went dark.

CHAPTER 3

"Mom, mom what happened?" Ricky asked. Not being able to see a thing frightened him. "Mom?"

"I'm not your mother," a voice said in the darkness, a girl's voice.

"My mom was right next to me when everything went dark. Mom!" Ricky shouted.

"I don't think you are where you were."

"What are you talking about? Who are you? It's too dark for me to see you."

"My name is Lexus. I've only been here a few minutes longer than you. What were you doing right before everything went dark?"

"I tossed a coin into--"

"I knew it!" Lexus interrupted.

"What do you mean?"

"Just before everything went dark for me, I also tossed a coin into Lake Espeth."

"I didn't toss my coin into a lake. I tossed it into a small fountain at Disney World," Ricky said.

"I don't know where that is, but I think our tossing the coins into the water caused our coming here."

"Where's here?"

"I have no idea," Lexus said. "Do you know why we have been brought here?"

"No," Ricky said. He still didn't believe he had gone anywhere. He wondered if he was dreaming.

"Even if you don't know any more than I do, I'm glad you're here. I didn't like being here alone in the dark," Lexus said.

"Yeah, I wouldn't want to be here alone either."

"I think we're in a cave," Lexus said. "Maybe it's one of the large caves in the Repoth Mountains."

Ricky wondered what country Lexus was from and where the Repoth Mountains might be.

"Now that my eyes have adjusted to the darkness, I think it's a little lighter in that direction," Ricky said.

"I too see an area that looks lighter than here, but since I can't see you or where you're looking I think we need to hold hands before we start going anywhere."

Ricky paused before answering. He wasn't comfortable holding a girl's hand, especially the hand of a girl he didn't know. However, he knew what she said made sense. "I suppose you're right."

A hand brushed his arm, and he found it in the darkness. Her hand felt soft, but she had a firm grip.

"We better watch where we walk or we may step off a ledge or walk into a wall," he said.

"I agree," Lexus said. "By the way, what's your name?"

"Ricky."

Suddenly someone screamed barely a dozen feet from them. Lexus seized Ricky's arm with her other hand, and he found himself grabbing onto her. The scream came again in the form of a terrifying high pitched wail.

The screaming changed to a voice. "Help! Help me!"

"It's okay! Calm down," Lexus said.

"Who's there?" the new person asked. "I can't see a thing!"

"There are two of us here. We don't know how we got here either, or why we're here," Ricky said.

"What were you doing when everything went dark?" Lexus asked.

"I tossed a coin into the river rapids by my house."

"I knew it," Lexus said. "What's your name?"

"Bebo, what's yours?" Bebo still sounded frightened.

"I'm Lexus."

"And I'm Ricky. Do you know where we are?"

"I don't have any idea what happened or where we are," Bebo said. "I want to go back right now!"

"We all do, but I don't think we can right now. We were going to walk over to where it looks like there's a little more light," Ricky said.

"Where's that? Everything looks pitch black to me."

"I wonder if we should wait here to see if anyone else is coming," Lexus said.

"I guess we could, but how would we ever know when the last person arrived?" Ricky asked.

"You arrived a couple of minutes after I did, and Bebo, you got here a couple of minutes after Ricky. I think if we wait another two or three minutes we should know if anyone else is coming or not."

"Okay," Ricky said.

"I hope my sister is okay," Bebo said.

"What do you mean?" asked Lexus.

"She was with me when I threw the coin into the river."

"My mother was with me," Ricky said, and for the first time since his arrival thought about how worried she must be.

"My cousin was with me," Lexus said. "It may be important that someone was with each of us when this happened, but I think they are still back where we left them."

"I think you're right," Bebo said. "The coin had my name on it, not my sister's."

A shiver shot up Ricky's spine at Bebo's mention of his name on the coin.

"My coin had my name on it," he said, and the realization that the coin actually contained a magic that must have had a purpose in transporting him to this spot finally sunk in.

"You mean we all threw the coin into water at the same time. That seems incredible," Bebo said.

"I don't think we had to have thrown the coins in at the same time. The only thing we know is that the coins brought us all together here at the same time," Lexus said.

"How do we get back?" Bebo asked.

Neither Lexus nor Ricky answered. They didn't know either.

"I think what we need to do first is to find our way out of this darkness," Lexus said.

"I agree," Ricky said. He realized he and Lexus were still holding hands.

"Come to my voice Bebo and hold my hand so we don't get separated in the darkness," Lexus said.

"Is that you?" Bebo asked from just a few feet away. Ricky thought Bebo must be short because the voice sounded like it came from someone who wasn't much taller than his own waist.

"Yes," Lexus answered. "Oh, you are a little one."

"What are you? A giant? Don't squeeze my hand so hard."

"Okay, Bebo, I'm sorry if I startled you," Lexus said.

Ricky thought her voice sounded calm and comforting.

"I think we should start walking now. I'm worried that the little light that is over there will fade," Ricky said.

"Lead on," Lexus said, and the three started walking.

They walked slowly to avoid falling into a crevice, but other than stubbing their toes on a handful of scattered boulders, they soon arrived unharmed in a section of the cave where they were able to see a few feet in front of them. They had travelled in silence, but now that they could each make out the others' silhouettes they began to talk.

"Where are you two from? You are both giants!" Bebo exclaimed. He pulled his hand out of Lexus' grasp.

"Tall or not, we're still your friends," Lexus said.

"That's right. I don't want to hurt anyone," Ricky said. He stared at Bebo who couldn't have been any more than three feet tall. "Why did you say we were giants? We're normal size. Certainly you've seen hundreds of others who are like us."

"Not where I come from. How tall are you?"

Ricky couldn't tell who he asked, but he answered anyway. "I'm five feet five."

"How old are you, Ricky?" Lexus asked.

"I'm fourteen years old."

"I'm five feet three inches tall, and I'm almost fourteen," Lexus said.

"Well I'm thirteen, and from where I come from, I'm tall for my age. Something tells me we're not from the same worlds,"' Bebo said.

"What?" Ricky asked.

"I think he must be right," Lexus said. "If those coins were magical, we could have all been brought here from anywhere."

"You mean this might not be earth?" he asked.

"Or Shantell," Lexus said.

"Or Criax," Bebo said.

"At least you and I look alike," Ricky said to Lexus while the realization that they may have come from separate worlds sank in.

"I wonder about that," she replied.

Ricky stared at her and wondered why she said that. In the gloom he could make out her silhouette: two arms, two legs, hands, feet, a head with two eyes a nose and a mouth. He couldn't tell the color of her hair or for that matter her skin, but that didn't matter to him anyway.

Lexus pulled her hand away from his. "It's not polite to stare."

"Excuse me," he said. "It's not polite where I come from either."

"I think the light is brightest in that direction," Lexus said.

"I hope that means there is a way out of this place," Bebo said.

"There must be a way out. It makes no sense that the coins would bring us here without a reason," Lexus said.

Ricky hadn't thought about it, but now that Lexus mentioned it, he figured there had to be a reason the three of them had been brought to this place.

"I can't imagine what the three of us could do that would be so significant. Maybe there is no reason behind our being sent here other than the magic in the coins," Bebo said.

"You mean like the coins were cursed, and it was our misfortune to have found them?" Ricky asked.

"Yeah," Bebo said.

"Did your coins have a number on them?" Lexus asked.

"Yes," Ricky said, "mine said it was number 12 of 51."

"Mine was 11 of 51," Lexus said.

"And mine was 13 of 51."

"It might explain the order we arrived," Ricky said.

"It could," Lexus said. "Since number ten wasn't here when we arrived and number fourteen didn't show up after us, it could mean those coins had another purpose. Hopefully, someone here will be able to explain to us what's going on."

"You mean if there's anyone else living in this place," Bebo said.

"Listen," Ricky said softly. He could hear the sound of what he thought was a large flock of birds taking flight.

"Birds?" Bebo asked.

"I think so, but I can't hear them anymore," Ricky said. "Did you hear them, Lexus?"

"I'm not sure," she said. "Let's hope they're not birds of prey."

"Birds of prey?" asked Bebo. "You mean birds that hunt people? We don't have anything like that on Criax."

"We have many species of birds where I come from. Most are harmless, but we have two types that are very dangerous. Only a few people live in the regions where those birds live," Lexus said.

"Luckily on Earth we don't have any birds like that," Ricky said.

"Maybe they don't have them here either, but the quicker we find daylight the better I'll feel," Lexus said.

"Well, it's definitely lighter ahead," Bebo said, and the three started walking again.

After they travelled another quarter mile, daylight began to filter through the gloom.

"I knew it," Lexus said.

"What?" Ricky asked. He turned and looked at her, seeing her clearly for the first time. He tried to say something, but for the moment, he remained speechless.

CHAPTER 4

"**A**m I that ugly? You know, people don't exactly look like you on my world either," Lexus said.

"No, no, you're not ugly at all. In fact, I think you're very pretty. It's just that I've never seen a person with blue skin or blue hair before."

"This is the only color we come in on my world," Lexus said. "I've never seen a person not blue, so you are a little hard to get used to, too."

"I think you both look weird," Bebo said. "What's all that stuff growing out of your head?"

"You mean our hair?" Ricky asked. "Don't you all have hair where you come from?"

"No, only the animals have fur or hair. We have evolved past that."

Ricky wanted to make some witty comment about how silly Bebo looked but decided not to say anything that might hurt his feelings. He already felt sorry for Bebo. The guy looked feeble and stood less than four feet tall. His shiny bald head looked out of place on such a young looking face. Ricky realized Bebo didn't have eyebrows or eyelashes either.

The three of them stood there for a few seconds studying each other.

"I think this clinches it. We are all three definitely come

from different worlds. The fact that we can understand each other interests me," Lexus said.

"The same magic that brought us here must have something to do with that," Ricky said.

"I think so, too," Lexus said.

"I wonder why the coins selected the three of us?" Bebo asked. "I don't have any special skills, other than being slightly taller and smarter than most the kids my age."

Ricky smiled at Bebo's comment about being taller than his peers.

"I'm also a second cousin to the King's family, but I've never heard of anyone a young as me being selected for the diplomatic corps. One of the princes is also named Bebo. Maybe the coin found me by mistake."

"Did the coin have your last name on it?" Ricky asked.

"Yes, that's true. The coin did say Bebo Thill, and my last name is different than the King's."

"I'm fairly certain that the coins were meant for us. However, I also can't say why. Like you, Bebo, I have no special skills, although I'm a good climber. Perhaps the coin picked me because I'm a girl, and you two needed a leader."

"Since when have women been in charge of anything?" asked Bebo.

"On my world, the women are generally accepted by all as superior over men. Is it not the same on your planet?" Lexus asked Bebo.

"Ha! Not at all. Men run things."

They both looked at Ricky as if to break the tie.

"I don't think I'll be much help to you. On my world women and men are usually considered equals," Ricky said. He wanted to add that in his house his mother seemed to be the boss but decided that would only confuse things. Besides, he knew his dad usually gave in to be nice or to avoid his mom being angry with him.

"I like that," Lexus said. "Let's be equals since we're all in this together."

"Okay," Ricky said, and they looked at Bebo.

"Oh alright, although it sounds like I'm the only one who comes from royal blood," Bebo said.

"I wonder how long we'll be here or if we'll be able to find food or water in this place," Ricky said.

"I think we'll be out of this cave pretty soon. Maybe we'll see something once we're out," Lexus said.

A number of small cracks and fissures in the cave wall above them let in a little light, and up ahead the cave looked like it opened up to the outside. They walked for another ten minutes before finally breaking out into the open.

"How beautiful," Lexus said.

"Fascinating, but also a little scary, don't you think?" Ricky asked Lexus.

"Yes."

Ricky looked at their surroundings. They appeared to be in a large valley surrounded on three sides by steep rock cliffs and by a vast sea on the fourth side. The sky was blue, but Ricky did not see any clouds or a sun. From the shadows on the cliff wall directly in front of him a couple miles away, he figured the sun was either rising or setting behind the mountains that contained the large cave from which they had just escaped.

The ground around them consisted of rock and sand, but he could see trees and other vegetation in the distance.

"At least we're out," Bebo said, "but this isn't exactly a paradise."

"Too bad there are no people here who could help us," Lexus said.

Ricky looked at her in the bright light. The color of her skin matched the blue in the sky, and her hair, cut short with a lot of waves, was a much darker navy blue. Her eyes matched her hair. Despite being blue, Ricky thought, she was still very pretty. She wore very loose fitting, Khaki pants and a white, short sleeve sweater.

"You're staring again," she said.

"Sorry."

"It's interesting that our clothing is similar," Lexus said. "We all three have pants and tops on. While our shoes look different, we're all still wearing something to help protect our feet."

Ricky noticed she wore black boots and Bebo had on leather sandals. Bebo's leather shorts and vest looked strange to him, but he understood what Lexus had meant. His own tennis shoes, blue jeans and a brown tee shirt might look a little strange to them.

"What should we do now?" Bebo asked.

"Should we go down to the water and see if we can drink it?" Lexus asked.

They agreed and walked toward the sea. The ground became sandier, packed at first, and then softer as they neared the shoreline. Ricky noticed that the sea had small waves that reminded him of the beaches in Florida. He found the similarities reassuring. He also noticed some birds flying in the distance and pointed them out to his two companions.

Closer to the water they started seeing shells and the occasional skeleton of a fish. Bebo ran the last ten yards to the water's edge and capturing some water in his hands, he tasted it.

"Cold, but it tastes a little strange. I suggest we don't drink much of it now. If we drink just a little we can see if it makes us sick."

"On earth we can't drink the sea water. It's too salty," Ricky said.

"We can drink all the water on our planet, but sometimes we have to clean it first," Bebo said. "I'm not sure if I know what you mean by "salty", so you'll have to taste it yourself."

Lexus approached the water alongside Ricky, and they both tasted the water. To Ricky's surprise, he didn't taste any salt in the water. He thought the water had a slight mustard flavor, but as he liked mustard, he didn't mind.

"I think it's okay," Lexus said. She started to lean down for another sip when a large claw broke the surface of the water and reached for her.

"Lexus!" Ricky shouted and grabbed her. He pulled her away from the water just as the claw ripped into the sand where she had been.

Another claw appeared and then the head of a sea creature Ricky had never seen before. The monster surged onshore almost the entire fifteen feet length of its body. Its pincers snapped and reached for Lexus and Ricky as they ran away from the shoreline.

Once the creature realized the two were out of its reach, it slithered back into the water.

"Wow! What was that?" Bebo asked. He had scampered back with the others.

"Looked sort of like a giant shrimp with huge claws," Ricky said, "but I've never seen anything like it before."

"Me neither," Lexus said. "I think it wanted me for its lunch. Thank you for saving my life."

"You would have done the same for me," he said.

"If I wasn't too terrified to move."

"There goes our drinking water," Bebo said.

"We may find more water elsewhere, and I think we could always come back here. We'd just have to be very careful," Lexus said.

"I suggest we see if there is a way out of this valley," Ricky said. "The mountains run right out into the sea, so if there's a way through them it's not along the shore."

"And I'm not swimming in that either," Bebo said. "Not with those things out there."

"The thing we saw might be one of the little ones," Ricky said.

They walked away from the beach and toward the green vegetation in the distance. As they did, they noticed the shadows from the sun setting behind the cliffs had grown. Nightfall would come soon.

They walked quickly and finally reached the first of the bushes and small trees.

CHAPTER 5

The vegetation around him looked similar to the plants back home, but Ricky thought something about them was different. The leaves on some of the plants looked much thicker than any of the plants that grew in the Everglades, but he imagined that the plants that grew in Africa or Asia might have thicker leaves than those in Florida, too. They smelled good, and he thought about how they would attract the bees back home.

"That's it," he said.

"What's it?" Lexus asked.

"I haven't seen any insects here."

"Now that you mention it, I haven't either," she said.

"As sweet as these plants smell, the bees back home would be all over them," Ricky said.

"I'm not sure what you mean by 'bees'," Bebo said. "I find it interesting that every now and then one of you use a word that I don't understand."

"Don't you have insects on your world?" Lexus asked.

"Yes, that word I know," Bebo said.

"Maybe you don't have bees," she said.

"We don't," Bebo said. "At least, nothing comes to my mind when I hear the word."

"Interesting," Lexus said.

Ricky looked at Lexus, but she didn't say anything else. Ricky thought she had to be very smart. She seemed to figure things out faster than anyone he had known before.

Bebo reached up to a large, shiny leaf and started to tear a piece off.

"Ouch!" he screamed and pulled his hand back. He looked at his hand, and Ricky could see it had already started swelling and turning red. "Ow! That burns!" Bebo started rubbing his hands together.

"Don't do that," Ricky said.

"Ow! Now this hand burns, too."

"I thought that's what might happen when you rubbed your hands together," Ricky said. "It's like poison ivy. The stuff irritates whatever it touches and rubbing it only spreads it around."

"But it's green," Bebo said.

"Does the color matter?" Lexus asked.

"Of course," Bebo said. "Only the red and orange bushes are supposed to be dangerous."

"Maybe on your world, but obviously not here," she said. "On Shantell, we don't have any dangerous plants."

"I want to go home," Bebo said. "I don't like it here." He sat down on the ground and rubbed his eyes, but Ricky didn't see any tears.

"Don't rub your eyes until your hands are clean," Ricky said.

Bebo jerked his hands away from his face.

"We all want to go home," Lexus said soothingly. "I'm sure there was a reason we were brought here, and I'm just as sure that after we fulfill our purpose here, we will be returned home."

"I hope so," Ricky said. He sat down next to Bebo. "This place gives me a bad feeling, and I already miss my mom. She must be awful worried about me."

Lexus sat down with them. "I was supposed to go to Gorth tomorrow. My whole family is going. It's supposed to be a fun vacation. I don't suppose they'll go now. When I get back, I suppose my little brother will be quite mad at me."

"Gorth?" Ricky asked.

"It's a beautiful place in the mountains. There are lots of things to do and so much to eat."

"That's what I want to," Bebo said. "I'm hungry, but if you can't eat the plants here what can you eat?"

"Just because one plant might be poisonous, it doesn't mean they all are. In Boy Scouts they taught us to watch what the animals eat. That's how you can find out what's edible," Ricky said.

"That doesn't help much. The only animal I've seen tried to eat you and Lexus."

"I think Ricky's right, Bebo. Look up there."

They both looked up in a nearby tree.

"That little creature is eating some dark berries," Lexus said.

"Looks like the prairie dogs we have back home," Ricky said.

As they watched a second, similar looking animal approached the first, and they shared the berries.

"I don't see any other berries anywhere on that tree," Bebo said.

"It probably picked the berries from somewhere else and took them there to eat," Ricky said.

"Then I think we should look around and find them," Bebo said.

Lexus nodded at Ricky, and the three stood up and started their search. They didn't have to look very long as Lexus found several clumps of similar berries hanging from a nearby bush.

"Only eat a couple at first. Then, we should wait a while to see if we get sick before eating the rest," Ricky said.

"I thought you said if the animals ate them, then we could eat them," Bebo said.

"That's usually the case, but not always. Besides we can't be sure these are the same berries."

"I think Ricky is right. Let's only eat two for now and then wait a while," Lexus said.

Bebo shook his head, but only popped two into his mouth. "They taste good."

Lexus and Ricky did the same.

"It'll be dark pretty soon. The shadow has climbed up to the top of the cliffs," Lexus said. "We'll need to find someplace to spend the night."

"How about right here?" Ricky asked.

"I think somewhere else might be better. It's too open here."

"What do you mean?" Ricky asked.

"Remember what you said about the little creature taking his food up into the tree?" Lexus asked.

"Yes."

"The small animals on my world also do that. They do that because larger animals will take their food away. It's something they have learned over the centuries. It also implies there are larger animals out here. We have not seen any, but that does not mean they are not here."

Ricky knew that she was right. "That makes sense, but I haven't seen anywhere that might be a place to hide."

"Not yet," she said, "but up ahead the vegetation gets thicker, and there are more trees. We may find a place up there."

Ricky glanced over at Bebo and saw that he had already eaten all his berries.

"Well, at least we should know in a few minutes if the berries are poisonous," Lexus said.

"Come on, Bebo, we need to go a little further before it gets dark," Ricky said.

The three walked, and by the time Lexus and Ricky had eaten all their berries, the vegetation had become thick around them.

"This will make our journey a little harder," Lexus said.

"Ouch!" yelled Bebo. "Look out, these bushes have large thorns."

"They sure do," Ricky said. "Are you alright, Bebo?"

"Yes, but why do I have to be the one that always has to get hurt?"

Ricky couldn't help but grin. "Have your hands healed from that plant you touched?"

"Yes. Whatever was on that leaf only made my hands burn for a minute or two, but I wouldn't want to touch that leaf ever again."

Lexus walked over and studied the thorn bushes.

"There are actually a lot of these thorn bushes here," she said and started walking around them.

"Luckily it didn't break off in my hand," Bebo said. "The last thing I need here is an infection."

Ricky watched Bebo squeeze the spot where the thorn poked him and saw a little drop of brown fluid ooze out of the wound.

"Is that from the plant?" Ricky asked.

"What this? You mean you've never seen blood before?" Bebo asked.

"My blood is red," Ricky said.

"Well, you're strange," Bebo said. "I bet her blood is blue."

They had been following Lexus around the cluster of thorn bushes.

"Of course it is," Lexus said. "That's why I'm blue."

That didn't make sense to Ricky, but he figured a lot about his two companions and this world didn't make sense.

"This might work," Lexus said. "Come here you two and hold these two vines away from me, so I can get in there and check it out."

"Why do you want to go in there?" Bebo asked.

"I want to follow this narrow path in and see if there is an area in the middle of all these bushes that we can use for a camp tonight. The thorn bushes should protect us from any large predators."

"Predators?" Bebo asked. "I didn't think about that. Do you think there's any chance we might be sent home tonight? I don't think I like it here."

The two boys took the two large vines and pilled them away from the path. Lexus entered with caution and within a few steps turned to the left and disappeared from view.

"Be careful," Ricky said.

"I think we can make this work," she said.

"You go first," Bebo said. "Your vine wraps across high enough so I can avoid it. I'll let this one fall back in place after I get through the opening."

One sticker snagged Ricky's shirt, but within seconds the

three were standing together in a small eight by ten foot clearing surrounded by thorn bushes five feet high. A few vines crossed the space.

"I think we can move these out of the way," Lexus said. She grabbed one of the vines and placed it in a tangle of other vines on one side of the clearing. She carefully wrapped one end of the vine around some of the others to hold it in place.

Ricky and Bebo grabbed a couple of vines and copied Lexus' technique in securing the vines to the other plants. Soon, they had the clearing free of thorns and the three sat down on the soft moss that covered the ground.

"Now if I could only have a big salad," Bebo said.

"I'd like to have a hamburger," Ricky said.

"Whatever that is," Bebo said.

"Don't you have hamburgers where you come from?" Ricky asked.

"I'm not familiar with what a hamburger is, but when I hear you say it I get a vision of a sandwich with meat in it."

"Beef."

"We don't eat animal meat," Bebo said. "Besides being disgusting, it's against our beliefs."

"So everyone on your world is a vegetarian?" Ricky asked.

"That's right. If it's green and grows, we eat it," Bebo said.

"How about fruits and flowers?" Lexus joined the conversation. "On our world the fruits and flowers come in all colors. We eat many of them despite the colors."

"Nope, only green things."

"How about the dark berries you just ate?" Ricky asked. "They weren't green."

"Green plants don't burn my hands on my world. I'm smart

enough to know I'm not on Criax anymore, and I was hungry."

"Then maybe this hamburger of Ricky's might be acceptable to you now?" Lexus asked.

Ricky knew she was teasing Bebo. The little guy did come across a bit arrogant.

"Never," Bebo answered. "Civilized people don't eat meat."

CHAPTER 6

Darkness came quickly in this strange world. Fortunately, the temperature remained warm and the night peaceful. Ricky didn't fall asleep right away. He worried about his mother and whether he would ever see his parents again. He knew Lexus felt sure that they would be returned home after they completed whatever task brought them here, but his own doubts persisted.

He had pinched his arm more than once since his arrival in an attempt to wake from what he hoped was just a bad dream. Ricky knew being here scared him, and he was thankful for his two companions' presence. He couldn't think what it would be like if they weren't here.

Lexus, in particular, had a soothing effect on him. She was smart and seemed to be able to put things in perspective faster than anyone he had ever known. He had gotten over the initial shock of her blue skin and blue hair. In fact, he had to admit that she was very pretty.

For all their differences, Ricky had already started thinking that he and Lexus were pretty much alike. Bebo, however, was the odd one. The more he thought about it, the clearer it became that Bebo's size and lack of hair weren't the reasons he thought of him as being different. Bebo's personality and attitude toward things set him apart. He could not remember once where Bebo said we or us. Still, Ricky thought that having two other people with him on this adventure was better than only one.

At some point in the evening, he fell asleep. A rustling in the bushes nearby woke him. The sky showed some early signs of a sunrise, but on the ground it was still dark. He looked around, but other than Lexus's eyes looking back at him he couldn't see anything out of the ordinary. Lexus placed her whole hand to her lips. Ricky knew she meant for him to be quiet. He heard the noise again. Somewhere near their thicket of thorns, one or more large animals were moving about. After a minute, Ricky could hear the animals walk away.

"Hopefully, whatever they were, they're like Bebo and only eat green vegetation," Lexus whispered.

"Maybe the animals here don't eat meat," Ricky said.

"I wouldn't count on that. The giant crab sure seemed like it wanted to eat me," Lexus said.

"Yeah, I guess you're right. Think we'll find a way out of this valley today?" Ricky asked.

"I hope so."

"We'll need to find some water and food soon, too. The berries tasted good, but we'll need to find something else to eat."

"We should be able to," Lexus said. "Ricky, do the people where you come from live in family groups?"

"Of course."

"We live in families, and I think from the remarks Bebo made yesterday, he does too. I find it interesting that we come from different worlds, but we are all very similar. I'm sure the coins somehow made it so we could understand each other. I doubt that we speak the same language, but our appearances haven't been altered," Lexus said.

"I find this all hard to understand," Ricky said.

"Me, too."

"I didn't see a moon last night, but this world may have one. Does your planet have a moon?" Ricky asked.

"We have two. They're beautiful when they're next to each other."

"We only have one," Ricky said. "Does your planet rotate around a sun?"

"Yes. In school, they taught us that if we were to encounter others like us in the universe, then it would make sense that they would come from a planet similar to ours. I guess they were right. Of course, when I get back home, I doubt if anyone would believe me if I told them about you and Bebo."

"They would think I was crazy."

"Yet we are here," Lexus said.

Ricky pinched his arm again, and nothing happened.

"Yes, we are," he said.

The sky became lighter, and Ricky stood up and stretched. He saw a large flock of birds in the distance.

"More birds over there," he said.

Lexus stood and looked. "I imagine this world will have a wide variety of animal life. This valley is somewhat isolated. Maybe only a few species can get in here."

"Let's just hope we can get out," Ricky said.

"Should we wake up our friend?" Lexus asked.

Rather than answer, Ricky gave Bebo a gentle shake.

"Wake up," he said. "It's morning."

Bebo mumbled something and sat up.

"Where's my salad?"

"Sorry, Bebo, we all have to look for our own food today," Lexus said.

"Why so early?" Bebo asked.

Ricky looked at his watch. He knew what time it was back on earth, but he couldn't be sure about the time here. "We only had seven hours of darkness. Maybe the nights here are shorter."

The two stared at Ricky. He could tell they were trying to understand what he said.

"Interesting," Lexus said. "I understand that to be a period of time, but it doesn't really equal any term we use. Somehow, however, I understand that seven hours is equal to about a third of your world's daily cycle of day and night."

"That's right," Bebo said. "Sort of like yesterday when you mentioned that meat sandwich."

"The hamburger," Ricky said.

"Yes," Bebo said.

"I guess it only makes sense that the days on each of our worlds have their own distinct durations, and how we measure that time could be different," Lexus said.

"I don't care," Bebo said. "I'm hungry. Let's get something to eat."

The three left their thorn sanctuary and resumed their trek. They hadn't gone far when Ricky spotted some green plants that reminded him of cabbage. The tops had been chewed off.

"These might be what the animals we heard last night were eating," he said.

"Looks leafy on the outside, but it's almost like a bread on the inside," Bebo said. He yanked a piece of the bread-like interior off the plant and popped it into his mouth. "Tastes good."

"There are a lot of these plants around," Lexus said. "I think we should eat a little now, but bring a bunch with us for later."

"I'm going to eat a bunch right now," Bebo said as he put another handful in his mouth.

"Well, I think Lexus is right. We don't know for sure how any of this stuff will affect us. It's best to eat just a little at first," Ricky said.

Lexus and Ricky nibbled on a little bit and placed larger portions in their pockets. Ricky noticed that Lexus' pockets were actually pouches sewn onto her slacks. Bebo ignored their advice and continued eating.

"That was good," Bebo said. "Now, how are we supposed to get out of here? We're surrounded by cliffs and sea."

"There must be a way through," Lexus said. "We can't go by sea, and we could see most of the cliff wall on the side we came from. There were no plants to hide any passages through the cliff wall back there. Remember? We looked and didn't see a way through back there."

"Well, at least I won't starve," Bebo said.

"Come on," Ricky said, and the three started walking.

Soon they came to a small stream with crystal clear water. The stream posed no obstacle to their travel as it was shallow and barely a yard across

"Must be flowing off the cliffs and going to the sea," Ricky said. He knelt down and scooped some water up with his hands. "Hey! Did you see that?" He let the water spill from his hands.

"Yes, but what were they?" Bebo asked.

"Like hundreds of miniature star fish and in a bunch of different colors," Ricky said.

"They were beautiful," Lexus said. "They must hide in the loose soil at the bottom of the stream. When you reached into the water, you frightened them and they fled. They didn't go very far, though." She reached into the water a couple of feet downstream, and the star fish again dashed away. "Tiny, beautiful creatures."

Ricky saw Lexus smile as she watched the star fish. He cupped his hands, filled them with water from the stream, and drank. Unlike the water in the sea, this water tasted like the water back home. He pulled the chunk of the plant out of his pocket and started eating it. He had to agree with Bebo, it tasted quite good.

Lexus and Bebo drank from the stream as well. After Bebo finished drinking, he stuck his entire head in the stream for a second. He pulled it out and shook it, spraying water over Lexus as he did.

"Oh, that feels better," he said.

"You could have waited until I was finished drinking, or at least moved away," she said.

Her remarks didn't seem to bother Bebo.

CHAPTER 7

They crossed two more small streams before they reached the base of the cliffs.

"There's no way we can go up and over them," Ricky said.

"I'm a good climber, but I think you're right. Going over them is not a choice," Lexus said. "Unfortunately, the bushes grow right up against the base of the cliffs. We could walk right by a passage through the mountains and not see it."

"Maybe we were supposed to stay in the cave," Bebo said.

"You want to go back to that dark cave and just wait for something?" Ricky asked.

"Not by myself," Bebo said.

"If we can't find a way through these mountains, we may have to try your idea. For now, though, let's walk along the cliff wall toward the sea and see if we can locate a way through. It's not far, and I'd rather double back from there than go all the way around the other way just to come back here if we don't find a passage."

"Makes sense to me, Lexus," Ricky said.

The three started their search. Ricky thought the sea was no more than a few hundred yards away.

"The bushes are really thick," Lexus said. At times they had to walk around thick patches of bushes, some with nasty thorns.

"Why didn't we check out that tunnel?" Bebo asked.

Ricky and Lexus stopped and looked at Bebo.

"What tunnel?" they both asked.

"The one we just passed."

"Show us," Lexus said.

Bebo took ten steps and pointed at the cliff wall. Ricky and Lexus looked but saw nothing but solid rock or thick bushes. Ricky realized Bebo's perspective was about a foot and half lower than his, so he bent over and looked again. In a gap between branches and leaves he saw an opening in the rock that appeared to lead into a tunnel. Until they cleared away the bush that blocked the entrance, they wouldn't be able gain access to it.

Ricky stepped back, allowing Lexus to lean over to take a look.

"It's definitely worth checking out. Great discovery, Bebo," she said.

"I don't think we can get to it until we chop down this bush," Ricky said. The bush looked like one that might be used in a hedge back on earth. It stood about six feet tall and spanned a similar distance. Other plants, some similar and some not, grew on both sides of the one that blocked the tunnel. Without tools Ricky didn't know how they were going to remove it.

"I found it," Bebo said. "You can rid us of the bush."

Ricky didn't like Bebo's attitude. In fact, he was starting to not like Bebo at all.

"You know, this bush doesn't have any thorns. We may not need to kill it," Lexus said. She squirmed through a few of the branches. The branches didn't bend easily, and Ricky could see that Lexus struggled to make progress toward the opening. Rather than continue toward the tunnel, Lexus surprised Ricky by starting to climb the bush.

With so many branches to work her way through, Lexus made slow progress. Fortunately, she only had to climb a few feet before the bush started to bend under her weight. Ricky realized what she was trying to do and jumped up, grabbing the top of the bush as it leaned his way. He forced the top of the bush downward. Together, he and Lexus bent the bush away from the cliff wall and the opening.

"Bebo, can you look into the opening and see if it leads anywhere?" Lexus asked.

Bebo sat on the ground watching them work, but did get up and checked out the opening.

"It looks like it leads to a passageway deeper into the mountain. There's also some light in there," he told them.

Lexus smiled at Ricky. "Maybe this is our way through," she said.

"I hope so, but how are we going to get off this bush and into the tunnel?"

"I hope you don't mind, but since you're heavier than me, I think I should go next while you're still holding down the bush. That'll make it easy for me, but you'll have to work your way around to this side of the bush once I'm off."

As Lexus crawled off the bush, Ricky had to put all his weight on it to keep it from popping back up and blocking the entrance. Despite the bush being pulled aside, Lexus still had to maneuver herself through a number of smaller branches from other plants before she entered the tunnel.

"I'm in," Lexus said.

Ricky had a plan, but he knew it wouldn't be easy. He had placed his entire body on the large bush to keep it down, but his head faced the bottom of the bush. Before he could try to get from the bush to the cave, he first had to rotate his body to get his feet pointing to the ground. He needed to do this without losing control of the bush. He worried that if the bush managed to return to its upright position, he would have a very difficult time bending the bush by himself.

He swung one leg to his left. The bush didn't move, so he swung his other leg to the left. That's when his plan fell apart, and everything happened at once. The bush bolted back to its upright position pushing Ricky into a tangle of branches and leaves. He found himself hanging in an angle, his head lower than his feet. Fortunately, two things saved the event from being a total disaster. He had stopped falling with his head inches above the ground, and when he stopped, he was looking directly into the tunnel.

"Ha! Ha!" Bebo laughed.

Even Lexus had a hard time suppressing a grin. "Need help?"

Rick managed to untwist his arms and get them free, but his body slipped down a couple inches when he did. His head now brushed against the ground.

"If you could pull my arms, I think I might be able to slide out."

"Come here and help me, Bebo," Lexus said.

They brushed aside the branches that reached into the tunnel, and each grabbed one of Ricky's arms. They pulled, and Ricky wiggled his way free of the bush.

"Thanks," Ricky said brushing the dirt and leaves off his

clothes. "I hope this is the way through. I'd hate to have fight that bush again to get out of here."

"You did well, Ricky. Without you we might not have been able to make it into here, and without you, Bebo, we wouldn't have seen the entrance." She looked down the tunnel, "I think this is our way through."

"Not very high, is it?" Ricky asked when he stood and bumped his head on the rock ceiling.

"Just for you," Lexus said. The couple inches difference in their height allowed Lexus to stand almost straight up.

Bebo grinned at her comment.

"The vegetation growing on the sides appears to be giving off just enough light for us to see," Bebo said. "We don't have any plants back home that produce light."

"Only this one type of plant is producing the light. Let's hope that this plant grows throughout the tunnel," Ricky said.

Ricky's discomfort in having to lean over while he walked only lasted for about thirty yards. The tunnel expanded in both height and width and brightened with the increased vegetation growth on the walls.

"This is more like it," Ricky said.

The three walked in relative comfort for another ten minutes before they came to a spot where the tunnel forked into two tunnels.

"Which one should we take?" Bebo asked.

"What do you think, Ricky, the one on the right?" Lexus asked.

"It has a red stone in the wall directly above it. It might mean something, so let's take it."

The three entered the right tunnel. The tunnel shrunk in size shortly after they entered it, and once again, Ricky had to duck his head down to avoid bumping it on the ceiling. Less vegetation grew on these walls and therefore, less light illuminated their way.

"I hope we don't have far to go," Ricky said.

"Look at that," Lexus said and pointed to a tunnel about three feet in diameter that led off to their right.

Ricky had a clear view into the dark tunnel as its base started about four feet above the ground. Bebo had to jump up to look into it.

"Too dark," Bebo said. "I'm not going in there."

For once Ricky agreed with him, but he didn't say anything.

They continued walking, and before long they discovered another tunnel. About the same size as the first one, this tunnel also opened through the wall on their right. They only paused briefly at this tunnel, and in another minute they encountered a third small tunnel that cut through the wall to their right.

"Something tells me that one of these is our way out," Lexus said.

"Let's keep going," Bebo said. "We can always come back here if we hit a dead end."

After another five minutes, the tunnel opened up into another larger tunnel.

"This is better," Lexus said.

"I don't know," Ricky said. "Look at this." He pointed at another tunnel entrance a few yards to their right. At the top of the tunnel entrance was a red rock. "I think we just went around in a circle."

"Ahhgh," Bebo sighed.

"I think we need to check out the three smaller tunnels we

saw inside," Lexus said.

"Too dark," Bebo said. "You can crawl through them, but I won't."

"I will, if you won't, Bebo, but it would be easier for you to explore them," Lexus said.

"Here," Ricky said. He pulled some of the fluorescent vegetation off the wall and handed it to Bebo.

"Well, maybe," Bebo said, but the light faded out. "Nope, no way."

"Wait a second," Lexus said. She went over to a nearby spot on the wall, and after a second, she returned with a piece of the vegetation still attached to a thin layer of rock.

They watched the small plant for a full minute before agreeing it would continue to shine.

"The roots need to remain attached to the rock for it to produce the light," Lexus explained.

Ricky found a section of the wall covered with the light producing plant. He worked on a piece of the rock wall until a section nearly a foot long and almost as wide came off. The rock separated from the wall in a thin layer and was surprisingly not heavy at all.

"Come on," Lexus said, and the three reentered the tunnel marked by the red rock.

When they reached the first of the three smaller tunnels, they still had to persuade a reluctant Bebo to enter it. When he finally agreed, Ricky lifted him up and helped him crawl into the tunnel. He took the small piece of vegetation that Lexus had brought along. Ricky placed the larger piece in the small tunnel's entrance behind Bebo. The light enabled Ricky to see inside the tunnel to the point it curved to the left, about twenty feet away from the entrance.

Bebo started to go around the bend in the tunnel when he stopped and returned to the entrance. Ricky was about to ask him what was wrong, when Bebo picked up the larger section of vegetation and dragged it back with him to the bend in the tunnel. He set the larger piece down, before disappearing around the bend.

"Maybe we should have brought more of the plant," Ricky said. "It's not as plentiful around here, just enough so we can see."

"How's it going, Bebo?" Lexus called out.

Bebo didn't answer.

"I hope he's okay," she said.

"I'm sure he is," Ricky said. "He hasn't been gone long enough to have gone far."

"Bebo!" Lexus shouted.

"Quit shouting. It echoes in here," Bebo whined as he reappeared around the bend. "This tunnel only goes a short distance before it hits solid rock."

Ricky helped him out of the tunnel, and the three continued on to the next tunnel.

"Can't someone else check this tunnel?" Bebo asked.

"Guess I could give it a try," Lexus said while she scrambled into the entrance without any trouble. Her body filled a lot more of this tunnel than Bebo had in the previous one.

Lexus had trouble reaching back and taking the larger piece of vegetation from Ricky.

"Lexus, let Bebo do this tunnel, too." Ricky said.

"I did the last one," Bebo said.

"Bebo, I'll do it, but I think I'll have to back out if I come to a dead end. It would be easier for you," Lexus said.

Ricky stared at Bebo and waited patiently for a response.

"All right," he said. "You know if you two weren't giants, you could be doing this instead of me."

Lexus backed out of the tunnel, and Ricky boosted Bebo up and into the tunnel. Bebo used both pieces of vegetation to light his way through the tunnel. This time the tunnel had multiple turns, and Bebo stayed out of sight for quite a bit longer than before. He also took both lights with him. After he disappeared from sight around the first bend, it wasn't long before the residual light from the plants faded to darkness in the part of the tunnel Ricky could see from the entrance.

"I imagine if the plants stopped giving off light, Bebo would be shouting and rushing out of the tunnel in a hurry," Lexus said.

"That's for sure," Ricky said. "I guess it's just a longer tunnel. Although, it wouldn't surprise me if he's just around the first bend taking a nap."

"Me either," she said. "Ricky, I'm glad you're here with me. I don't mean I'm glad you were taken away from your home. I'm not glad that happened to either of us, but since I'm here, I'm happy that the coin selected you, too."

Ricky tried to think what to say. Lexus impressed him with her calm attitude and her high intelligence, but he'd never been very good at talking to girls. However, he had to admit to himself that her presence made being here in this strange world a lot less frightening.

"I guess I feel the same way about you. I--"

"Hey, I think this way leads out!" shouted Bebo from inside the tunnel, cutting short Ricky's remarks.

"You think?" asked Lexus. "Does it, or doesn't it?"

"There is an opening to the outside. I just can't tell if it's on the other side of the mountains or on the side where we came in."

"That would be a bummer," Ricky said.

"You can get through," Bebo said looking at Lexus, "but I don't know about you."

"Too narrow for me?" Ricky asked.

"At the very end, it gets tight for the last few feet. You might be able to find another way out," Bebo said.

"What do you mean?" Lexus said.

"You and I can do whatever we've been brought here to do. We really don't need him," Bebo said.

"The three of us stick together, Bebo. We don't abandon anyone," she said.

"If you insist, but don't blame me if you get stuck," Bebo said.

"I won't," Ricky said with less confidence than he sounded.

"Follow me," Bebo said, "but you can't really get lost." Bebo still had the smaller light in his hand.

Lexus climbed into the tunnel. "I assume the plants provide lighting ahead, but you may want to bring another plant since you'll be behind us."

Ricky grabbed a small loose rock with a small piece of the light producing vegetation and followed Lexus as she crawled through the tunnel. The tunnel reminded him of the play areas at some of the McDonald's back home. He kept close to Lexus, and other than when she slowed to pick up the light producing plant that Bebo had left on the tunnel floor, the three moved quickly toward the end of the tunnel.

"Be careful getting out. We seem to be on the side of a steep hill. There's a ledge but it's not very big," Bebo said.

Ricky couldn't see past Lexus and couldn't tell if Bebo had reached the exit. So far, the tunnel hadn't narrowed, so Ricky had no trouble following the other two. The tunnel took a sharp right and continued on.

"Oh, it's not too narrow. You should be able to make it through," Lexus said.

Outside light now brightened the tunnel, and Ricky watched as Lexus disappeared around a bend to the left. He crawled forward and watched Lexus squirm through a narrow opening to the outside. She made it through without much effort.

"Getting out without falling down the hill is the hard part, but we'll help you," Lexus said.

The first real fear struck Ricky since the moment of his arrival to this strange world. If he couldn't make it out, he would have to back all the way out of this tunnel. His knees were already sore.

"Come on, Ricky. We'll help you," Lexus said again.

"Okay, coming through," Ricky said as he started to squirm through the small hole. He stretched his arms out in front of him. He clawed forward with his hands while he pushed with his feet. He couldn't bend his legs to get any traction making his progress slow. Lexus grab his hands just as he became stuck.

CHAPTER 8

"Stop pulling," Ricky said. "I need to try to spin my body around a bit."

They had helped him to the point that his head was half out of the tunnel, but the rest of him remained stuck inside. Ricky grunted, strained, and finally succeeded in twisting his body a little.

"There, I think that should do it. Can you pull me out a little further?"

Lexus grabbed one arm while Bebo grabbed the other. They pulled, and Ricky pushed as hard as he could with his feet. His body slowly slid out far enough for him to use his arms.

"Thanks guys. I think I can do the rest myself," Ricky said.

"Be careful you don't tumble out. You could get hurt," Lexus said.

Ricky looked down the steep drop of about twenty feet.

"Maybe you should guide me, but if I fall, don't fall with me," Ricky said.

"Don't worry. I won't," Bebo said.

Both Lexus and Bebo stood on a ledge that looked to only be a foot wide. The ledge only extended a few yards on either side of the tunnel. There appeared to be a number of divots and jutting rocks along the rock wall that he could use to hold onto as he eased himself out of the tunnel. They would also make getting down rather simple.

Ricky's biggest dilemma while getting out of the tunnel was to keep his head above his feet. This meant he had to start climbing the side of the cliff as soon as he could bend his body at the waist. With Lexus help, though, he made it out safely.

"Now," Bebo said, "how are we going to get down?"

"Oh, Bebo, this looks easy," Lexus said. She started down the side of the cliff and reached the ground with ease.

Ricky considered himself a good climber, but Lexus amazed him with her skill at climbing down the steep rock wall.

"I can climb," Bebo said, "but this is pretty steep and a long way up."

Ricky guessed Bebo's size affected his perception of just how high they actually were.

"Come on," Ricky said. "I'll help you."

The words had barely gotten out of Ricky's mouth before Bebo leaped onto Ricky's back.

"Hey! Be careful, or we'll both go tumbling off this." Ricky thought Bebo was surprisingly light, even for his size. However, climbing down turned out to be harder than it should have been because Bebo kept moving around on Ricky's back affecting his balance.

When the two reached the safety of the ground, Bebo scrambled off Ricky's back.

"Took you a lot longer than it took her," Bebo said. "Next time I'll go with you, Lexus."

Ricky looked at Lexus and rolled his eyes. She did her best to suppress a smile.

"We are definitely not back in the valley," Lexus said. "Now that we're out, I wonder which way we're supposed to go."

"Good question," Bebo said. "I'd like to get this over, so I can go home. I wish the coin would've left a map or a set of instructions for us."

"Since we don't know which way to go, we might as well start walking anyway we want. I'm guessing the coin will take us where we're supposed to go," Ricky said.

"Then why no map?" Bebo asked again. "You have more faith that we'll get some kind of sign than I have."

"Help! Help!" A voice shouted nearby.

"I think we just got our signal," Lexus said. "The voice came from that direction. Let's go."

"It may be dangerous," Bebo protested, but as the other two had already started moving, he followed them.

The terrain took on an appearance not unlike the Everglades. If he hadn't just crawled out of a mountainside, Ricky thought he could almost imagine being back home. The ground changed from being rocky and dry by the cliff to wet and spongy as they moved deeper into the thick underbrush.

"Help!" The voice sounded close, and the person sounded more frightened.

"Hang on!" Ricky shouted. "We'll be there in minute."

"Hurry, but be careful."

"Why should we be careful?" Lexus called out.

"The ground is full of mud traps. If you step in one, the mud tries to drag you under."

"Quicksand," Ricky said to his companions.

"I understand," Lexus said. The three slowed down and walked more cautiously toward the voice.

"Where are you?" Lexus asked.

"Over here!"

Ricky looked to his left. The person sounded like he couldn't be more than a few yards away. He took a couple of steps toward the voice.

"Down here!"

"There he is," Bebo pointed toward a spot on the ground.

Through the leaves of an odd looking plant and half hidden by some tall grass, Ricky saw a small head poking out of the ground and a mud covered arm that held onto a narrow branch. The branch had already cracked under the person's weight, and looked like it might break off at any moment.

Lexus was the first to him and stepped into the quicksand. Fortunately, she was only a foot or so from solid ground, and with Ricky's help she scrambled out of the mud without too much effort.

Ricky lay down on the ground and reached out for the trapped boy's muddy hand. They brushed fingers, but Ricky couldn't get a grip. Ricky slid out further until his chest, shoulders, and head were just above the quicksand.

"Sit on my legs," Ricky said to Lexus and Bebo. He needed their weight to prevent his being dragged into the quicksand during his effort to pull the boy out.

They understood and jumped on top of his legs. Ricky stretched out his right arm as far as he could. He grabbed the boy's hand just as the limb snapped, and the boy started sinking. He pulled with all his strength, and the boy, realizing he had a chance to escape, pulled on Ricky. For a second, Ricky didn't know if he could save the boy or not. The boy's other arm came out of the mud and grabbed Ricky's arm. He slowly began to pull himself out of the quicksand.

However, as the boy's rescue progressed, Ricky realized he

was in a dangerous predicament.   When the boy got close enough, he flung one of his arms around the back of Ricky's neck. When he did this, his weight pressed Ricky's face down into the wet mud. Ricky fought to keep his face up, but the boy continued climbing on top of him. The weight on him became too much until it finally pushed Ricky's entire head into the quicksand.   Ricky strained against the weight. He wanted to yell for him to get off but couldn't. He didn't know how much longer he could hold his breath.

All at once, the boy was no longer on his back, and Ricky jerked his head out of the sticky mud and breathed. Lexus pulled him by his shirt and helped him sit up.

"Are you okay?" she asked.

Ricky thought that she might have tears in her eyes. "Yes. I'm fine, but that was a bit scary," he said. "How's he doing?" Ricky looked over at the boy. For a moment he thought his eyes were playing tricks on him. "Is that fur?" he whispered to Lexus.

She nodded. "Never seen anything like it. Have you?"

Ricky shook his head.

The boy sat under a large bush with his knees up and his arms wrapped around them. He looked terrified. Bebo stood off to one side and watched the boy. The boy wore pants of some sort, but the mud that covered them prevented Ricky from telling their color or the type of fabric from which they were made. He thought the boy wore a sleeveless shirt but again the mud hid its details.

"Are you okay?" Lexus asked the boy. Her voice sounded soothing. Ricky thought some of the tension faded from the boy's face.

"Who are you?" he asked. He stared at his three rescuers.

"I'm Lexus, this is Bebo, and the young man who pulled you out of the mud is Ricky. How are you?"

"I'm fine, thanks to you," he said it to all three, but his eyes acknowledged Ricky. "I thought I was going to die. That would have been terrible."

"For you," Bebo said.

Lexus gave Bebo a stern look.

"No, I don't mean it that way. Sure, I didn't want to die, but it's more important that I reach the Temple of Facall before it's too late."

Lexus asked, "What's your name? Why do you have to go this Temple of Facall?"

Instead of answering the question, he looked at each of them for a moment. "You three are not from this world. I've never seen people who look as strange as you three. This is a part of our world we never visit, but I've never heard tales of mutants here."

"Hey, don't be calling us mutants, fur face," Bebo said.

"Bebo, please," Lexus said. "We're not from this world. Each of us is from a different world, and we are not yet sure why we've been brought here. Are you alone?"

"Yes. I'm Vincent Wollitzer," he said and paused to study their expressions. When none of the three gave him any indication that they knew who he was, he continued. "I was flying to the Temple of Facall to be anointed as leader of this world. The aircraft I was on had an explosion. I don't know if a mechanical failure caused the explosion or a bomb."

"So you thought we might be on the side of your enemies?" Ricky asked.

"No, not really. I have no enemies, or at least, none that I know of. That is why I was selected to rule," Vincent said.

"Where is your aircraft now?" Ricky asked.

"It's not far from here, but it burned up in the crash. The pilot and my aide died in the crash. My safety capsule allowed me to eject from the plane just before impact. The pilot tried to land but crashed into the trees. I don't know why my aide did not leave in his safety capsule, but I found his body near the wreckage, too."

"Won't there be a search going on for you?" Ricky asked.

"Oh, I'm sure there's one going on right now, but they'll never look for me here. We were going around some bad weather when the explosion occurred. The plane turned around to return to our home airfield. Our radio no longer worked, and we cut across this territory in an effort to shorten our return trip. Usually no one flies over this section of our planet. We may be a thousand miles from where they expect us to be."

"A thousand miles!" Bebo said. "We could never walk that far."

"Oh, there's an outpost only hundred or so miles from here, but we can't get out of here," Vincent said.

"Why?" Lexus asked.

"Unless you know how to climb several hundred feet of sheer rock, cross vast stretches of quicksand, or hold your breath long enough to cross a mile of sleeping gas, there is no way out."

"I think we're all good climbers," Lexus said.

"I don't think you're that good," Vincent said.

"My guess is his rescue was not why the coins brought us here," Bebo said.

"Coins?" Vincent asked.

"It's a long story," Lexus said. "We'll tell you, but first please tell us a few things. Unlike Bebo, I feel like you might be the reason the coins brought us here. Why do you feel that it's urgent for you to be anointed ruler?"

"Our world is large, but there are only two nations that rule it. Both have roughly half the world's land within their borders. The population of each nation is about the same. For some silly reason, the two nations have always distrusted and disliked each other. Despite this animosity, the two nations have existed in peace for nearly three hundred years. There have been a few small skirmishes and a lot of name calling, but no actual warfare."

"That sounds better than my world, Vincent," Ricky said.

"But if I don't get to the Temple soon, I'm afraid both sides will blame the other for my disappearance and war may break out," Vincent said.

"Why?" Lexus asked.

"For hundreds of years, representatives of both nations have selected a teenager from my land to rule the world. It's mostly a ceremonial title, but I would resolve conflicts and disputes."

"How would you do that?" Ricky said.

"By proclamation. I would listen to each side's arguments and issue a decree that they would follow. In many ways I would be more a judge than a ruler. I don't interfere with each nation's internal politics," Vincent said.

"Why do they select someone so young?" Bebo asked.

"I am young, but I went through a screening process. Each nation had to agree that I was their choice."

"But why didn't they pick someone older?" Bebo asked.

"The hope is that I can rule for a long, long time. The small gaps between rulers are when the threat of war is at its highest. If they picked an older person the gaps would come more frequently."

"Makes sense to me," Lexus said. "Why do they choose the leaders from your people? Don't your people reside in one of the two nations?"

"Not really. There are three very small regions that are located in the border lands between the two nations. They aren't large enough to provide a buffer zone, and for as long as anyone can remember, neither nation has had any interest in these regions. The regions are separated from each other by thousands of miles. My region is one of the three."

"Like a neutral nation," Ricky said.

"Yes, but we are too small to be considered a nation," Vincent said. "I'm still confused. If you're not from this world, how do you speak my language?"

"Like I said, it's a long story, but I guess now is as good as ever to tell you," Lexus said.

The three sat down next to Vincent and told him their stories. By now, the three were in agreement that the coins brought them to this place and allowed them to understand each other. While they agreed that there had to be a reason why the coins sent them here, they weren't sure what that reason was. None of the three had any idea how they were supposed to return to their homes.

"I understand that the nations in your world don't like each other, but why do you think your absence will cause a war?" Lexus asked. "Can't they simply elect another person in your absence?"

"Each side will blame the other for my disappearance. It is illogical, neither side has any animosity toward me, but they let their emotions rule their behavior. The chances are that rather than agreeing to start another search for a new ruler, they'll start yelling at each other. They'll work themselves into a war fever and violence will break out across their borders. Millions may die."

"Vincent, I think we've been brought here to get you back to your people," Lexus said.

"I think Lexus is right," Ricky said.

Ricky and Lexus looked at Bebo. He seemed reluctant to say anything.

"Yeah, maybe so," Bebo finally said.

"But how?" Vincent said. "There is no way out unless you have a flying machine."

"We don't have an airplane, but I think between the four of us, we can do it," Ricky said.

"Yeah, now that you're here, you can show us what's safe to eat," Bebo said to Vincent.

Lexus looked at Ricky and shook her head. Ricky grinned. He knew Bebo had a hard time thinking of anything but himself.

<h1 style="text-align:center">CHAPTER 9</h1>

"Eating is never a problem," Vincent said. "You just need to find what you like."

"Maybe you can point it out for us," Bebo said in a sarcastic voice.

"Well, it's all around us," Vincent said. "We eat the plants. Some taste better than others, but you can eat any of them."

Bebo broke off a leaf and popped it into his mouth. "Yuck!" he exclaimed and spit it out.

"I don't care for that one either," Vincent said. "Here, try this." He plucked a large yellow flower off a bush and handed it to Bebo.

Bebo took a small bite, chewed on it for a few seconds, and then popped the rest of the flower into his mouth.

"I guess that one tasted better," Lexus said to Ricky.

Bebo plucked another flower off the bush and started eating it.

"I don't know how we can get out of this territory," Vincent said, "but I'm willing to show you the obstacles that block our escape."

"Good," Lexus said.

"First, I think I'll try to get some of this mud off me," Vincent said. He walked over to a nearby tree whose branches sloped close to the ground. The branches had several large curved leaves. Vincent tipped a leaf toward him and water poured out of it onto him. Without pausing, he walked over to a second and then a third leaf, and poured more water onto himself.

"That's like taking a shower," Ricky said. He poured the water out of one leaf over his face and arms to wash off the mud that had gotten on him during the rescue of Vincent. The water was cool but not cold.

It took Vincent longer to get the mud off him, because it covered most of his body. While they waited for Vincent to finish, Ricky studied Vincent's appearance. He had been surprised by Lexus blue skin and hair, but he had seen people on earth whose skins were different colors. He even knew a girl in school who died her hair blue. Of course, she was sent home the first day she showed up in school with the blue hair, but he had seen it. Even Bebo, with his small size and total lack of hair, made him think of pictures he had seen on television of kids that were sick. Bebo did look different from them, but Ricky could relate the pictures with him.

Vincent, however, looked totally different from anyone he had ever seen. He had two arms, legs, hands, eyes, ears, etc., like humans, but light brown fur covered most of his body. The fur appeared to be about an inch thick. The fur did not cover portions of his face and the palms of hands, but it covered every other part of his body that Ricky could see.

"Can we drink this water, too?" Ricky asked. He motioned toward the water trapped in the bowl-shaped leaves.

"Of course," Vincent said.

Ricky bent the edge of a nearby leaf and drank a little of the water as a small amount poured out. Lexus walked up to him, and he held the leaf while she drank.

"If you're ready, we should go," Ricky said to Vincent.

Vincent led, and the four began their trek. The trees and bushes thinned out, and Ricky could see high mountains to their left and the ocean off in the distance to their right. The prairie appeared to go on for miles in front of them.

"This isn't bad," Bebo said. "The ground is flat and soft to walk on. Vincent, is the weather always this nice?"

"No. This time of year, it is usually warm like this, but we have a lot of storms. Later in the year it gets cold."

"Like earth," Ricky said.

"And my world," Lexus said.

"Vincent, don't you have any ships or boats that sail the oceans?" Ricky asked.

"Only a few foolhardy people venture out into the oceans. They are full of sea serpents and giant creatures that have ended the lives of most who have tried to explore the seas. We do have boats that sail on our lakes and rivers, but not the oceans."

"Why did you think there might have been a bomb on your aircraft?" Lexus asked.

"I don't think there was a bomb. In fact, I'm almost certain there wasn't a bomb, but since I don't know what caused the explosion, I can't rule it out."

"Have many of your kings been assassinated?" Bebo asked.

"You mean world rulers, like I'll be, if we ever get out of here?" Vincent asked.

"Yes, because a lot do in my world. By the way, you and I are the only ones here who have royal blood in our veins," Bebo said.

"There is one incident in our history of a world ruler being assassinated, but that happened long, long ago," Vincent said.

"Sounds like your world is more peaceful than mine," Bebo said.

"I don't know. Within the nations there are problems with crime. Small border skirmishes between the two nations are also common. We aren't as peaceful as you might think."

"Wouldn't your brother or cousin be next in line to rule if you don't return?" Bebo asked.

"No, not at all. Rulers are not chosen among family lines. Every year a mix of six boys and girls, who have successfully moved into middle school, are selected in a screening process that is monitored and approved by both nations. These six serve as the pool of candidates from whom a world ruler would be chosen if something happens to the existing ruler."

"Fascinating," Lexus said. "In my world the six would be girls."

"In mine only boys would've been selected," Bebo said.

"In mine it would be a mix, too, I think," said Ricky.

Vincent listened but continued without comment to the others' remarks. "Since the selection is done with such routine, year after year, and a new ruler is only anointed once every eighty or so years, the process of selecting the six is done with boring simplicity rather than much excitement."

"I imagine that changes when it comes time to choose one out of the six to be the next ruler," Lexus said.

"Yes, but as a candidate I didn't see any of it directly. There is a lot of arguing and maneuvering within and between the two nations, but I wasn't exposed to it," Vincent said.

"Oh! Look at that," Lexus said.

The four stopped and stared at a fast moving river that

appeared ahead of them. They hadn't noticed it on their approach because the ground dropped down about thirty feet in front of the river and then sloped back up on the other side. From a distance they couldn't see the small gorge that cut through the otherwise flat terrain.

"You didn't tell us about the river," Bebo said.

"I didn't know it was here. No one has explored this land, or at least if someone did, he didn't live to tell the rest of us about it," Vincent said.

"Well, that's moving too fast for us to swim across," Bebo said.

"I think I could get across," Ricky said.

"You might," Lexus said, "but the rest of us wouldn't."

"We could follow it and see where it goes," Ricky said.

"The water has to flow into the sea. It's only a mile or two over there," Vincent indicated to their right. "We might find a place to cross by the sea if the water spreads out and gets shallow enough. Too close to the sea could be dangerous, though."

"I suggest we follow it, but head away from the ocean," Lexus said.

They all agreed and resumed their trek. After a mile, it became evident that the river ran straight toward the high mountains ahead of them.

"I'm afraid this river may have us trapped on this side of it," Vincent said after a while.

"You know," Ricky said, "I've been looking at some of these giant trees. A few have grown up right next to the river. Their branches in some spots extend out almost completely across the river. If we had a rope, we could almost swing across."

"Ha! You are a dreamer," Bebo said.

"The trees can supply the ropes. There are dozens of vines in them that wrap around the trunk and branches. You simply have to unravel them and cut them off where they're attached to the tree," Vincent said. "We play on this type tree all the time. I don't know why I didn't think of it."

"I'm a good climber," Lexus said, "but I've never swung on a vine or a rope before."

"It's fun, Lexus. I'll show you," Ricky said.

"Then I'm up for it," she said.

Bebo didn't say anything, but Ricky could tell he wasn't thrilled with the idea. Ricky didn't know if Bebo was concerned about climbing the tree, swinging on a vine, or both.

"The tree we passed back there," Ricky pointed at a tree about a hundred yards behind them. "That tree looked about as good as any I've seen. See that large branch," he continued pointing.

"Yes, Ricky, perfect," Vincent said.

The four ran to the tree. Without waiting, Lexus scurried up the tree and out to the middle of the branch that extended over the river.

"I've never seen anyone climb so quickly," Vincent said.

"Me neither," Ricky said.

"I see the vines you mentioned, Vincent," Lexus said. "Should I start unraveling one?"

"Yes, but be careful not to lose your balance," Vincent said.

"I'll come up to help," Ricky said.

"Me, too," Vincent said.

In a couple of minutes the three had a long, hardy vine unraveled.

"How are we going to break it off the tree?" Lexus asked.

"With this," Vincent held up a pocket knife.

"Is it sharp enough to cut through the vine?" Ricky asked.

"Sure," Vincent said. He pulled out a blade and the pocket knife started to glow.

"Is it a flashlight, too?" Ricky asked.

"It can provide a little light it the dark, but not much. It glows when it is opened and the blade is activated."

"So, it is more than a simple blade," Lexus said.

"Yes. Watch," Vincent leaned in close to the vine and pressed the blade against it. The blade cut through the vine like a warm knife cuts through butter.

"Awesome," Ricky said. He held onto the vine to ensure it didn't drop to the ground once cut.

"How are we going to secure it to the tree, now that we've cut it off?" Lexus asked. "It's too thick to tie."

"I think I can do it," Ricky said.

He crawled out on the branch as far as he felt was safe. He found a spot where two smaller branches grew out of the larger branch that supported him. He looped the end of the vine around the branch and did his best to tie the end in a simple knot. He could loop it around itself, but he couldn't tighten the knot. He continued wrapping the vine over itself and around the branch, alternating inside and then outside the two smaller branches. Finally, he pulled the vine snug against itself and the branch.

"Bebo! Try to catch the end of the vine when I toss it to you," Ricky shouted.

"There are too many branches to throw it through," Lexus said. "Give me the end of the vine and I'll climb down with it."

Ricky started to say that climbing down with the large vine in hand sounded like the harder way to do it, but he remembered how agile Lexus was when she moved around in the tree.

"Okay, be careful," he said.

He watched in amazement as she scampered around one branch after another on her way down. The vine had sufficient length to reach the spot on the ground where Ricky thought they should start their swing to the other side.

"I'll go first," Vincent said.

"No," Lexus said. "I'm certain the coins brought us here to help you return to your people. We need someone to go first to make sure the vine will hold the weight. We might be able to survive a fall into the river, but we might not."

"I can't expect one of you to sacrifice yourself for me. I'll go," Vincent said.

Lexus, however, had the rope vine and leapt off the edge. Gravity tugged at her, and the vine swung her across to the other side. Her feet caught the top of the ledge on the far side. She managed to maintain her balance without letting go of the vine.

"That was fun!" she shouted.

"I thought you hadn't swung on a rope before," Ricky said.

"That was my first time," she said.

"Could have fooled me. You did great," Ricky said.

"How do we get the vine back across?" she asked.

"Just throw it as hard as you can," Ricky said.

"If you can tie a rock on the end, it'll be easier to throw," Vincent said.

Lexus wrapped the end of the vine around a rock that

looked like a small brick and tossed it toward the other side. The rock fell out about two thirds across, but the momentum of the vine carried it into Vincent's outstretched hands.

"Got it," Vincent shouted and without hesitation swung across. Lexus grabbed him as he reached the other side.

"All right, Bebo, your turn," Lexus said.

Vincent tossed the vine across. A taller person could have caught it. In fact, Bebo might have caught it if he had stood near the edge. Bebo, however, stayed a full yard away from the edge. The vine swung back and forth over the river, out of everyone's reach.

"Maybe I'll wait here until you all come back," Bebo said.

"No way," Ricky said. "I have an idea."

Ricky climbed down the vine. As he did, he worried whether the vine might come loose. He had wrapped the vine over itself a few more times and thought it would stay secure, but he had placed his own weight on the vine while the others swung across. Now with him off the vine, would it still hold?

"What are you doing?" Lexus shouted.

"Give me a minute," Ricky said. He started to shift his weight back and forth. The vine responded, and Ricky swung towards one side of the river and then the other.

"Way to go, Ricky!" Vincent shouted when Ricky got a foothold on the bank near Bebo,

"Hop on," Ricky told Bebo. "Looks like I'm carrying you, again."

Bebo jumped onto Ricky's back.

"Now don't choke me this time," Ricky said and leaped into the air. He heard Bebo gasp as the vine initially let them fall toward the river. Despite his instructions to Bebo, he felt Bebo's arm tighten around his neck.

They swung across the river. Just as they reached the other side, Ricky felt the vine slip from the tree. His momentum carried them both to safety. As the two fell to the ground, the vine fell from the tree.

"That was close," Vincent said, as he and Lexus helped the two to their feet. "We won't be returning across the same way. There doesn't seem to be any trees along the bank on this side."

"Hopefully, we won't have to cross back over the river," Lexus said.

The four continued their trek. After another hour, they entered a forest where they paused to eat and relax. The afternoon sunlight broke through the trees and created a mix of bright spots and dark shadows that seemed to sway with the growing wind.

"Hope we don't get a storm," Vincent said. "There's not much shelter out here."

They continued walking and the weather worsened. Despite Vincent's remarks that there wasn't much shelter available to them, Ricky noticed that the ground was covered with twigs and small branches. He thought of the lean-to that he had made with his Boy Scout troop a year earlier. He had made one with less than half of the sticks and twigs that covered the ground around him.

"Are the storms here dangerous?" Ricky asked.

"Most of the time they aren't, but they can produce a lot of rain."

"How long before it starts raining?" Bebo asked.

"Don't know," Vincent answered, "but I think soon. I wish we had some place to hide from it."

"I have an idea," Ricky said. He described a lean-to and how it could provide a crude shelter.

"Brilliant," Vincent said. "I say we start preparing one now."

They all gathered as many long sticks as they could. Ricky started to explain the process of making a lean-to when he realized that Bebo was already working next to him. Lexus and Vincent continued to gather sticks.

"Have you done this before?" Ricky asked.

"No, but it sounded easy, and I'm good at making things with wood," Bebo answered.

Ricky noticed that Bebo's small hands nimbly placed the various sized and shaped sticks next to each other creating a perfect side to the lean-to. They worked so quickly together that Ricky decided to make it larger than he first intended. Lexus and Vincent joined them in the construction.

"Won't it leak?" Lexus asked.

"Yes, but if we put some leaves on top of the sticks it should help," Ricky said.

They put as many leaves as they could find on the lean-to while the wind began to howl. Most of the leaves blew off, but enough remained to deflect the rain. When the first handful of large rain drops hit them, the four scrambled under the lean-to. The last of the evening sunlight faded away.

"This turned out great," Lexus said. "Just getting out of that wind is a blessing."

"It's plenty big enough for all of us, too." Vincent said.

"We can thank Bebo for that. I think he built more of this thing than I did," Ricky said.

Bebo beamed. "It was nothing."

A loud crack of thunder startled them. Bright lightning

flashed in the sky. Ricky knew it wasn't safe to be under a tree during a lightning storm, but since they were in a forest with trees all around them he decided not to worry about their predicament. The intermittent rain turned into a heavy downpour, but after about twenty seconds it stopped. The wind continued to whip through the trees, and thunder echoed around them, but the rain had stopped. The four started a small campfire with some dry leftover sticks.

"That feels good," Lexus said rubbing her hands near the fire. "The air has gotten cool."

"It's nice to have the extra light, too," Vincent added.

CHAPTER 10

The four talked as the fire weakened. They used up what little dry wood they could find to keep it burning. Ricky wondered why he felt comfortable with this group. His anxiety about being here in this strange world had even diminished. He knew he should be more frightened. Deep down, however, he did worry about his mother, and what she must be thinking about his disappearance.

As the last flames flickered in the small fire, Lexus moved in closer to him.

"We'll stay warmer if we share our body heat," she said.

"I know," Ricky said, a little embarrassed. He let her snuggle against him. He noticed Bebo had already moved in close to Vincent, who had fallen asleep.

A loud roar that came from somewhere nearby woke them all. The sky had cleared, and the first hint of daylight stretched across the sky. Something growled, and they heard the loud roar again. Suddenly, the sounds of branches breaking and more growling erupted.

"Sounds like one animal is attacking another," Bebo said.

"And big animals, too," Lexus added. "What do you think, Vincent?"

"I hope they don't see or smell us," Vincent said. "I'm not sure, but I think it may be a torant fighting with one or more giant apes."

"Vincent, I understood you when you said giant apes, but what is a torant?" Ricky said.

"A large, nasty beast. Even the giant apes are no match for them," Vincent said.

"I understood him," Lexus said. "It must be because we have a similar creature on my world, and possibly you don't."

"They don't live anymore on our world, but they used to," Bebo said.

"Like our dinosaurs," Ricky said.

"Yes," Bebo said.

"Maybe we should leave now while it's preoccupied with the apes," Vincent said.

The sounds of snarling and even a few shrieks of terror echoed in the air.

"I think that may be a good idea," Lexus said, and the four stumbled out of their small shelter and continued their journey.

They had not gone far when Vincent stopped them and pointed to their left. "Be silent now," he said. He crouched behind the trunk of a large tree. The other three instinctively hid behind a small bush.

"Are those the apes?" Lexus asked.

"Yes, it appears they got away," Vincent said.

"At least those three did," Bebo said.

The forest had thinned out a little allowing Ricky to see three animals about a hundred yards away that looked like gorillas to him. The gorillas ran through the woods in the same direction Ricky and his companions were travelling. Nothing appeared to be chasing them.

"They didn't appear to notice us," Ricky said. "Are they

dangerous?"

"They can be. I learned at school that the large apes fall into the second group of animals," Vincent said.

"What does that mean?" Ricky asked.

"It means that if you leave them alone they will leave you alone. Like that bee on Lexus shoulder."

Lexus looked at her shoulder and smiled. She did nothing to chase it away.

"Those animals in the second group can be dangerous, but it is not in their nature to pursue and hurt people," Vincent explained.

The bee on Lexus shoulder flew away.

"You're braver than me," Ricky said to Lexus. "I would have overreacted and probably gotten myself stung."

"Ow! Ow!" Bebo shouted. "It stung me!" Bebo held his right hand in his left.

"You swatted at it," Vincent said.

"I don't like bees. Look at how my hand is swelling," Bebo said.

Ricky noticed that Bebo's hand had puffed up to almost twice its normal size.

"They're not poisonous," Vincent said.

"Maybe not to you," Bebo said.

"Let me look at it," Lexus said. She took Bebo's hand into hers and studied the area where the bee had stung him. With a quick pull, she removed the stinger. "That might help."

"I hope so," Bebo said.

"Here, eat this," Vincent said. He offered Bebo a funny looking spiral leaf.

"That's good," Bebo said. "Do you have more?"

"Over there," Vincent pointed at a small bush a few feet away.

Bebo hurried over to the bush and pulled off a leaf.

"Will that help with the bee sting?" Lexus asked Vincent.

"No. It'll just take his mind off the sting. I've noticed that boy likes to eat."

Ricky and Lexus couldn't help but smile. It hadn't taken Vincent long to see what motivated Bebo.

"You told us about group two animals in your world. I assume there is a group one?" Ricky asked.

"Yes," Vincent said. "Group one animals are those animals that pose no threat to people. Most animals in my world fall into group one. We also have a group three. Those are the animals that we learn to stay away from. They are savage beasts that will attack and even kill us. Most of those live in the oceans, but there are some that roam the lands."

"The torant is one of those in group three?" Lexus asked.

"Yes. Thankfully, I've only seen pictures of them and have heard recordings of their roar."

"Do you have a group four?" Ricky asked.

"No, just the three groups," Vincent said. "I do think we should keep walking. The further we separate ourselves from the torant, the safer we'll be."

Ricky tore off one of the spiral leafs and popped it in his mouth as the four started walking. It tasted sweet with a flavor of chocolate candy. He watched for another bush with the spiral leaves. When they passed one he tore off a couple leaves. He noticed that Bebo did the same.

"Lexus, try one of these. They are quite good," Ricky said. He offered her one of the leaves.

"Hmm, they are delicious. My mom warned me about boys that offer girls sweet things," she teased.

Ricky blushed. He knew she was teasing him, but he still blushed. He did like her. In fact, while deep down he yearned to be able to return to earth, he hoped there would be some way he could continue seeing Lexus. What would his mom say if he walked into his house with a girl with sky blue skin and dark blue hair?

"I'd like to be able to visit your world sometime," Ricky said.

"Remember, Ricky, girls are in charge in my world." She grinned again as she continued her teasing.

"Where girls rule and boys drool," Ricky said.

"What?" Lexus asked.

"It's just a silly phrase. It can be said either way to tease the opposite sex. In Bebo's case, he would say boys rule," Ricky said.

Ricky and Lexus continued talking and laughing about life as a teenager on their respective planets. Bebo and Vincent walked together with Vincent pointing out the various bushes and trees to Bebo. Bebo would occasionally pull off a leaf and taste it.

At one point, Vincent had them stop while a small herd of animals crossed in front of them. To Ricky, they looked like very small, prehistoric triceratops. About the size of large pigs, they moved at a steady pace until they were out of sight.

"What group are they in?" Lexus asked.

"Group two," Vincent said. "They travel with their young and are very protective of them. When they are alone, you can walk right by them, but with their young nearby they won't let you get close."

"Makes sense," Ricky said. He knew there were a lot of animals on earth that were like that.

Late in the afternoon the group walked out of the forest and into an open plain. They could see hills in the distance in front of them. Before the hills, a wide area of fog appeared to cover the ground.

"Wonder what causes the fog?" Bebo asked.

"I don't know," Vincent said. "But, if there is a way out, I think it has to be that way."

Ricky could see the ocean in the distance to their right and giant mountains way off to their left.

"Is the fog the sleeping gas you mentioned before?" Lexus asked.

"No. The gas is clear, which makes it all the more dangerous."

"We can always go down near the fog and follow it to the ocean to see if we can go around it," Ricky said.

"Or it may not pose any threat to us at all, and we can simply walk through it," Lexus said.

The four reached the edge of the fog after a steady thirty minute hike.

"It's pretty thick," Vincent said. "Do we want to try to cross here or try a different spot?"

"We know the fog doesn't go on too far because the hills we saw beyond them didn't have any fog around them," Ricky said.

A terrible roar answered their question for them.

"The torant!" Vincent screamed in fear.

Ricky saw it and for a second froze in fright. A large bear like animal with the head and mane of a lion stood about two hundred yards away. It stared at the four and roared again. Suddenly it dropped to all four legs and charged.

Ricky felt Bebo jump up on his back. He didn't try to knock him off.

"Quick! Into the fog!" Ricky shouted. He grabbed Lexus hand and pulled her as he ran into the fog. "Stay close, Vincent."

He had only taken a few steps when he stepped into quicksand.

"Stop! Quicksand!" Ricky shouted. He had one foot on dry land and pulled his other foot free. Vincent, who stood next to him, had to do the same.

"This way," Ricky said. He walked quickly along the edge of the quicksand. He stared at the ground watching for a spot where the quicksand ended. They needed to get deeper into the fog. The edge of the fog cleared every now and then for a brief second. That allowed them to look for the torant, but it also allowed him to see them. The torant stopped his charge about twenty yards from the edge of the fog. The fog thickened.

"The fog must concern him," Lexus whispered.

The torant roared as the fog around them thinned enough for the torant to see them. It roared again while it crept toward them.

"Come on," Ricky said. They came to a spot where it appeared the quicksand stopped, and Ricky led them deeper into the fog. Visibility dropped to only a few feet. Ricky had to lean down to watch where he stepped. He held on to Lexus hand and fought the urge to run. Before long, more quicksand blocked their way. Ricky again led them along the edge of the quicksand while he watched for a way around.

The torant roared. Ricky couldn't tell if the creature was closer than before or not. Did it follow them into the fog? Were they going in circles? Instead of moving away, would they pop out of the fog back near the torant?

The edge of the quicksand disappeared, and Ricky led the group in the direction he hoped would lead them out of the fog and nearer to the rolling hills.

"I hope we're going in the right direction," Ricky said.

"We are," Lexus said. The confidence in her voice reassured Ricky.

Twice more quicksand interrupted their trek, and each time, Ricky led them around it. Finally, they walked out of the fog and into the clear air.

"Okay, hop down," Ricky said to Bebo.

"I can't believe we made it," Vincent said. "Maybe I can make it back to civilization."

"Of course you will," Lexus said.

"Think that monster followed us?" Bebo asked.

"I doubt it," Lexus said. "It didn't appear to want to enter the fog."

"Still, it might be a good idea if we ran for a while to put some distance between us and the fog," Vincent said.

They agreed, and the four began to jog toward the hills and away from the fog. Neither Bebo nor Vincent ran very fast, so Ricky and Lexus had to occasionally slow to a walk for the two to catch up. After about ten minutes, Bebo said he was too tired to run any further.

Vincent looked back at the fog and said, "There's nothing following us. I guess we can walk."

"Look over there," Lexus said. She pointed in the direction of the ocean.

"Looks like smoke," Ricky said. "Should we check it out?"

"I don't know. No one should be living in here," Vincent said.

"Could it be a rescue party?" Ricky asked.

"Possibly," Vincent said.

CHAPTER 11

The four started walking and then jogged toward the smoke. Ricky could sense the hope they all had that they would find a rescue party. They ran up the gentle slope of a small hill. Ricky and Lexus ran side by side. They both came to a sudden stop when the origin of what they thought was smoke came into view.

"Stop," Ricky said in a hushed tone to Vincent and Bebo when they caught up. "Look!"

The four crouched and stared at the scene ahead. What they had taken for smoke was actually steam. A series of small geysers spewed hot water and steam out of the ground. Ricky counted five geysers in an area not quite as big as a football field.

What stopped them however, were not the geysers. Crawling in and around the geysers, they saw at least a dozen crab-like creatures, similar to the one that attacked Lexus and Ricky at the shoreline. A couple of the creatures looked huge, at least twice as big as the one that they had seen before.

"They must like the hot water," Bebo said.

"I didn't know they roamed so far from the ocean," Vincent said.

"It's only a hundred yards or so to the beach from where they are," Ricky said. "Maybe they find the geysers worth the trip."

"Obviously so," Lexus said. "I don't think seeing us would interest them at all at this point. Look, there's another one coming out of the sea."

Ricky saw another large crab-like creature emerge from the water and crawl toward the geysers.

"It's definitely not a rescue party," Ricky said. "We should keep trying to get out of here."

Vincent nodded in agreement. Disappointed, the four travelled on. By mid-afternoon, the group entered another dense forest. The thick vegetation and trees slowed them down, but Bebo, who had complained of the lack of food on the prairie, was ecstatic with the variety of food that now surrounded them all.

"The little guy sure likes to eat," Ricky said to Lexus.

"I think we've all said that before," she said with a smile.

"I know," Ricky said, "but it's hard not to say something."

They munched on a handful of blossoms and watched as Bebo hurry from plant to plant nibbling on each one as he did. Now and then he'd run back to Vincent and ask him something about a plant. Occasionally, he would spit out something that tasted bad. Finally, when he grabbed a leaf that burned his hand, he stopped.

"How do you know which ones to avoid?" he complained.

"You learn. If you were more patient and asked me before you grabbed everything, I could tell you," Vincent said. "Sometimes, we only eat the berries on a plant, or the flowers, or the leaves."

Bebo looked at Vincent, and Ricky wondered if Bebo was trying to decide whether slowing down his eating by asking a bunch of questions was worth it.

"And by the way, Bebo, the leaf you ate a while ago from the Dolox plant, we only eat when we have trouble going to the bathroom. I'm not sure how it will affect you."

Bebo looked back at the plants around him and tried to figure out which plant that was. He started to ask when he felt his stomach start to gurgle. His eyes widened, suddenly understanding what Vincent had said.

"Ahh!" Bebo half shouted and sprinted behind some bushes.

The three laughed out loud at Bebo's predicament. They sat down on the ground to rest and wait for Bebo.

"I hope we haven't been eating from the same bush," Lexus said.

"You haven't," Vincent said. "I would have warned you. Bebo was in too much of a hurry to listen to any advice."

"Will you know when we're close to the sleeping gas?" Lexus asked.

"I think so," Vincent said. "We have to cross a small mountain region---"

"Not those?" Ricky asked and pointed at the tall mountains to their left.

"No. We should see the mountains soon, I hope."

"You hope?" Ricky asked feeling a little frustrated. He felt Lexus' hand on his shoulder. He knew right away that she had put her hand there to calm him down.

"I'm familiar with the general geography of this area, but that's all. There are no trail markers or guide books. Like the ocean, we have given up on this part of our world centuries ago."

"Vincent," Lexus asked, "are there no natural resources in this region that might be important to your world?"

"There might be," Vincent acknowledged.

"Could you not fly into and out of this area with your airplanes?" Lexus asked.

"True," Vincent said. "It is a large area. If we make it out of here, I'll suggest our universities study the feasibility of inhabiting this area. I don't think anyone has thought about it in a very long time."

"Ricky, to get back to your question, I think we should be able to reach the mountains tomorrow. We should be able to find a way through them rather than over them. The valley of gas is just beyond the mountains."

"We'll make it through," Ricky said.

Bebo rejoined the group. He looked a little paler than he had before.

"Are you okay?" Vincent asked.

"I think so," Bebo said.

They started walking and hadn't gone far when Ricky sensed they were being followed. He looked around but didn't see anything. The sensation, however, got stronger, and after another minute he stopped and looked again.

"What is it?" Lexus asked.

"I don't know," Ricky said. "I feel like we're being watched."

They all looked around. The forest was thick and a mist had started falling, but they could see far enough to see if anyone or anything was out there. A movement up in the branches of a tree caught Ricky's eye. He looked up and studied the trees.

"Look at that," he said quietly.

His three companions looked up. At least a dozen monkeys stared back down at them.

"What group are they in?" Bebo asked. Ricky sensed the fear in his voice.

"I've never seen monkeys like them before," Vincent said. "They must be a rare or a new species."

"But are they dangerous?" Bebo asked.

"I don't know, but I don't think so. All the apes that I know of are in group two. Leave them alone and they leave us alone."

"They don't seem to be doing anything but watching us," Lexus said.

"No," Bebo said almost in a whisper, "they're watching me."

At first Ricky thought Bebo was imagining it, but then he realized that the monkeys closest to them were indeed staring at Bebo.

"You're the same size as them. Maybe they think you're one of them," Lexus said.

"Without the hair," Bebo said. "We have monkeys like them on my world, but they usually avoid contact with people."

"Most monkeys and apes here usually avoid contact, too," Vincent said.

"Let's keep walking and see if they follow us," Ricky suggested.

"Okay," Bebo said.

The four moved on, and the monkeys followed them.

"I think there are more monkeys now than before. They do seem to be fascinated by us," Lexus said.

"I don't like this," Bebo said.

"They haven't shown any signs of being aggressive. They seem to be curious, that's all," Vincent said.

"They may not be aggressive, but I agree with Lexus, there does appear to be a lot more now," Ricky said.

All four stared up into the trees. The monkeys stared back down.

"Maybe we should keep going and simply ignore them," Vincent said.

"Ahhh!" Bebo gasped.

Ricky looked at Bebo and saw what startled him. A four foot tall monkey with thick grey fur over its whole body, except for a small patch of red fur around one eye, stood on the ground only a few feet from Bebo.

"Stay calm, Bebo," Ricky said. "He doesn't look like he's threatening you."

"Put out your hand, Bebo," Lexus said softly. "He has something for you."

Ricky saw what Lexus had already figured out. In the monkey's right hand, Ricky saw a clump of leaves.

"Do it, Bebo," Ricky said.

Bebo cautiously put his hand out. The monkey took a couple of steps forward and offered the leaves to him. Bebo reached out and took the leaves. When he had them, the monkey retreated a few steps and climbed up the nearest tree.

What happened next surprised Ricky - Bebo took one of the leaves from his hand and put it in his mouth. When he did, the trees erupted with the monkeys cheering and jumping up and down.

"Vincent, I think your monkeys just gave Bebo a present," Lexus said.

"I think you're right," Vincent said. "Bebo, I don't know why they see you as a friend, but apparently they do. I think we can continue on with our trek now and not worry about the monkeys. In fact, I would think we could consider them our allies."

The four walked on with the monkeys following them. The further they travelled the more monkeys joined the group in the trees. They reached the end of the forest just as it was getting dark. They could see the mountains clearly now, as the terrain leading to them appeared to be a gentle rolling prairie.

"I suggest we spend the night here in the protection of the trees," Vincent said. "I don't think it would be safe to try to camp in open land."

"What about them?" Bebo said referring to the monkeys.

"I don't think they pose a threat to us at all," Lexus said. "They may actually warn us if a predator came our way."

"I think she's right. Let's camp right over there," Ricky said pointing to a spot where it looked like they could all have room to stretch out.

"Should we make one of those Lean-To things like we did before?" Bebo asked.

"It doesn't look like we'll get any rain tonight and the thick canopy of the trees will keep the morning mist off us," Vincent said.

"We shouldn't need one," Lexus said. "Vincent, what plants around here would be good for dinner?"

Vincent gathered some nearby flowers and leaves. Once he had plenty to share, the four sat in a small circle and ate dinner. They built a small fire in case the weather turned cool. By the time darkness had fully set in, the glow of the small fire was appreciated by all. They each talked of their home worlds.

Ricky listened and was amazed at the similarities in the four planets. Although different in appearances, the people in each of the worlds apparently behaved much like the people on

Earth. They all had family structures, schools for the young, local city and national governments, stores for shopping, farms, and even fads. Technology had evolved in different ways. Only Lexus' world had televised entertainment like Earth. In Vincent's world, the citizens had hand held devices that gave them the ability to see who they were talking to no matter the distance that separated them. Ricky mentioned that on earth they were just developing that technology.

"Why can't you talk to someone now?" Bebo asked.

"There is no antennae grid here. These have to be within a few miles of a relay antenna," Vincent said holding up his right arm showing everyone the bracelet he wore. "Except in this region and the oceans, we've had the antennae grid up and operational across our world for a very long time."

Ricky dosed off while Vincent and Lexus were still talking. Bebo had fallen asleep some time before. One thing Bebo had said stuck in Ricky's mind. Bebo said that the men on his planet could have two wives. At the time, Ricky hadn't thought much about it, but in his dreams he kept seeing himself trying to explain to his mother that he didn't want two wives. The dream didn't make any sense. Suddenly, the realization that something was moving nearby drew him out of his slumber.

He opened one eye and froze. All about them the monkeys moved quietly.

CHAPTER 12

It took only a second for Ricky to realize that the monkeys didn't appear to be doing anything malicious. Rather, they seemed to be curious. Some looked over others' shoulders, and some tugged at the monkeys that were nearest in order to swap positions and get themselves in closer.

Ricky noticed that a couple of the monkeys sensed that he was awake and backed away from him. He wanted to let them know he didn't mean them any harm, but he didn't know how. He watched them for a while before he fell back asleep. Something touched his arm, and he woke in a start.

"The monkeys," he mumbled.

"What monkeys?" Lexus asked. "They're gone."

He followed her eyes up into the trees and realized that they were no longer there.

"Last night they came out of the trees and were down here with us," Ricky said.

Lexus looked at the ground around them. "I see their tracks. That explains it."

"Explains what?" Ricky asked. He looked around and saw that Bebo and Vincent were still asleep.

"Look over there," Lexus said.

He followed her gaze and saw a pile of leaves, flowers, and berries.

"They left them for us," Lexus said.

"How about that? Awfully nice of them," Ricky said.

"Should we wake the others?" she asked. "It's getting light."

"I guess so," Ricky said. "Do you really think we'll be able to return home after we get Vincent back to his people?"

"Yes, I do," Lexus said. "I will miss you, Ricky."

"I'll miss you, too," Ricky said. He didn't know what else to say, so he stood up and stretched. "Vincent, Bebo, it's time to get up."

Vincent groaned, not wanting to open his eyes.

Bebo sat up right away and looked into the trees above them. "They're gone. Where'd they go?"

"We don't know," Lexus said, "but they left us some food."

"Wow!" Bebo said. He walked over to the pile and pulled a flower off the top. He popped it in his mouth. "Good," he mumbled. Bebo took a handful of leaves and started pacing around. He stopped and studied the ground around the area where he had slept. "Where are my shoes?"

Ricky looked around the ashes from the fire. He remembered seeing Bebo's shoes the night before. They weren't anywhere to be seen now. He remembered the monkey's visit to their campsite and their interest in Bebo.

"I think the monkeys took them, Bebo," he said.

"What?"

"Ricky's right," Lexus said. "They left the food, but must have taken your shoes."

"So all that food is mine?" Bebo asked. "Not a bad trade."

Lexus walked over to the pile and took a berry. "Do you mind?" she asked Bebo.

For a second, Ricky thought Bebo might protest.

"I guess not," Bebo said, "but don't take too much."   He returned to the pile and picked through and took all the flowers for himself.

By now, Vincent was awake and watching Bebo. He looked at Ricky and shook his head. Ricky smiled at Vincent and nodded.

Ricky and Vincent took a handful of leaves from the pile and ate them for breakfast. By the time everyone was ready to leave there was still a small quantity of leaves and berries left.

"Should we take the rest with us?" Lexus asked Bebo.

"Yes, but I don't have any room left in my pockets," Bebo said.

"We noticed," Ricky said. "How about if we put some in our pockets?"

"I guess that will be okay," Bebo said. "Don't forget, the monkeys gave that stuff to me."

The four left the campsite and in another minute were out in the open prairie. The ground was covered with what appeared to be a moss rather than grass. It felt soft and was easy to walk on.

"I guess they knew I didn't need any shoes," Bebo said.

"If we hit rockier ground, you'll miss your shoes," Vincent said.

"Then he'll just have to carry me," Bebo said.

Vincent looked at Ricky, but Ricky didn't say anything. He had gotten used to Bebo's pompous behavior. Plus, Ricky felt Lexus' gaze on him. He wondered how her words, her touch, and now even her gaze had a calming effect on him.

Their travel remained uneventful. By the time the sun beat

straight down on them, Ricky estimated that they had cut the distance to the mountains in half from when they started out that morning. In front of them, he could see that the moss on the ground yielded to a thick grass.

"This is interesting," Lexus said. "This strip of deep grass runs forever to both our right and left, but only appears to be about a quarter of a mile wide. Then it looks like the moss takes over again."

Ricky found it more interesting that he knew Lexus lips didn't say "a quarter of a mile", but that is what he heard. It reminded him of a foreign language movie he had watched the other night with his mom that had been translated into English. He could see that the characters lips weren't talking in English, but the voices that came out of the television were in English. He thought it funny at the time. Now, he was even more fascinated. Most of the time, it appeared that she and the others were speaking in English. Only when they used a term for which there was no equivalent in their own language did he see the disparity between the lips and the words. It must have been like that for Bebo, when he heard Ricky say the word hamburger on the first day they all arrived.

They reached the edge of the grass and paused.

"I don't like this. It's as tall as my knees," Bebo said.

"It's just grass," Vincent said. "I doubt if we'll run into anything dangerous in there."

"No snakes or alligators?" Ricky asked almost absentmindedly.

"The snakes on my world aren't dangerous, and the alligators or what we have here that I believe are similar to those you refer to are too large to be hidden in this grass. We do have rats, but I hope we won't find any," Vincent said.

"Rats! Yuck!" Bebo exclaimed.

"Let's go," Ricky said.

"Maybe we should run across," Lexus said.

They started jogging across the grass. To Ricky the grass felt thicker and stronger the grass back on Earth. It felt more like hay, but it wasn't hard to run in. They had travelled about a third of the way across when Bebo let out a yelp. Ricky looked back and saw Bebo brushing a couple of caterpillars off his leg.

The four kept running, but in a few seconds, Bebo howled again. He was bouncing on one leg and brushing the same type caterpillars off both legs. Ricky could see red blemishes appearing where the caterpillars had been.

"Here, Bebo, climb on up. I'll carry you," Ricky said.

Bebo didn't need any additional encouragement as he jumped onto Ricky's back.

They were nearly half way when Lexus shouted at Ricky. "They're on me now." She tried to continue running while she rolled up her pants and brushed off the caterpillars that had gotten up around her ankles and onto her legs. "Ow!"

Ricky noticed she looked wobbly.

"I'm getting dizzy. Don't let me fall, they'll get me."

"Get off!" Ricky said to Bebo.

"What?" Bebo asked.

Ricky knew he would have to carry Lexus. She was too big for Vincent.

"Here, Bebo, get on my back," Vincent said. "Hurry! I didn't think about the caterpillars. With our fur they really don't bother us, but I know they can sting."

Bebo grabbed Vincent and slid over to him. Ricky took

Lexus arm and helped her climb onto his back. He carried her piggy back style and jogged toward the mountains. She leaned forward and kept brushing the caterpillars off her legs. Ricky heard her crying softly to herself as she struggled to rid herself of the insects.

Ricky saw she was having trouble reaching one of the caterpillars, so he brushed it off for her. When he did, he felt a piercing sting in his little finger.

"Ouch!" he said. "Those are nasty critters."

He could clearly see the end of the grass field about a hundred yards ahead of him when he felt the first burning sensation on his legs. He ran faster, but a second and then a third sting ripped through his legs.

"Ahh!" he moaned.

"You've got to keep running, Ricky. My feet have gone numb," Lexus said.

He glanced up and saw she had tears in her eyes. A large drop emerged and rolled down her cheek. He thought of the pain she must be in. He would have to make it. Another series of stings almost made him trip and fall.

Lexus couldn't stop her tears, but she didn't cry for herself. She cried for this brave new friend of hers. She knew Ricky had to be suffering as much as she had, but rather than stop and try to get the caterpillars off his legs, he kept running for her.

Ricky noticed that even Vincent, who was a few steps ahead of him, had started swatting at his legs while he ran. Bebo frantically held on to Vincent's back.

The worst pain yet exploded in Ricky's right leg, and he screamed out.

"A little further, you can do it," Lexus whispered in his ear.

The end of the grass was only a few more steps, but his feet felt heavy, and his legs felt like they were on fire. He wanted to go to sleep, but when he looked down it seemed like all he could see were thousands of caterpillars looking back up at him. He could see their eyes, and then everything went black.

CHAPTER 13

The bright light hurt his eyes when he tried to open them, so he instinctively covered them with his hands. He tried to roll over, but his legs didn't want to cooperate. They felt like someone had placed heavy weights on his feet.

"How are you doing, Ricky?" a soft voice he thought he recognized came from the bright light.

"What happened?" he mumbled.

"Here, try to sit up and drink some of this," the voice said again.

A hand reached behind him and helped him sit up. Getting the bright light out of his face felt good. A hand tilted his head up slightly, and he felt water being dripped into his mouth. The haze in his mind started to fade away. He opened his eyes and had to blink a few times to get them to focus. Seeing the leaf and the blue hand brought him back to reality.

"Is everybody okay?" he asked in a raspy voice.

"Yes, thanks to you and Vincent," Lexus said.

Ricky saw Vincent off in the distance walking toward them and carrying something in his hands.

"He found a stream up ahead and has been bringing us back water."

"Is Bebo okay?" Ricky asked.

"Yes, he's just taking a nap. You were stung worse than the

rest of us," Lexus said.

"Oh yeah, those stupid bugs," Ricky said. He studied his legs. Dozens of ugly blisters covered both legs up to his knees. "Hey what happened to my jeans?"

"There right over there," she pointed to a spot right behind him. "We had to get the caterpillars off you, and we couldn't roll up your pants legs. You should wear looser fitting pants."

As if to illustrate the difference, Lexus stood up and pulled up one of the legs to her slacks. It slid up easily, and Ricky saw five nasty blisters.

"Don't make such a face, my legs aren't that ugly," she said.

"Not your legs," Ricky said before he realized she was teasing him. "The blisters, yours look a lot worse than mine."

"I must be more allergic to their poison than either you or Bebo. A couple even got through Vincent's fur and stung him. He said he's never seen so many caterpillars in one spot before."

"I can't feel anything below my knees. It's like my feet are asleep."

"The same thing happened to me," Lexus said. "In a little while, you should get the feeling back into them. Luckily, the terrible burning sensation doesn't return. The blisters are sensitive, but unless I touch the area, it doesn't hurt anymore."

"How bad were Bebo's legs?" Ricky asked.

"Not too bad. Either you or Vincent carried him most the way. I think he was only stung three of four times. He never lost the feeling to his feet." Lexus looked over her shoulder at Vincent. "I better go and see if I can help him."

Ricky watched her as she jogged off toward Vincent. He studied the blisters on his legs and counted over twenty. For the first time, he felt a little embarrassed to be sitting there in his underwear. However, he remembered the painful sensation from the caterpillars stinging his legs and knew that he would have ripped the jeans off himself if he could've gotten to those bugs.

"Glad to see you're up," Vincent said as he approached. "Do you feel your feet yet?"

"I think I'm starting to," Ricky replied. "How long was I out?"

"Not very long," Vincent said. "We should really start moving soon. I may be overreacting, but I don't like staying out in this open field too long. Right before we get to the mountains there's a bunch of trees and bushes. We need to get there before dark."

Ricky stood up. His legs and feet were still a bit shaky, but the pressure on his feet from standing seemed to help. He took a few short steps and sat back down next to his jeans. He looked in a pants leg.

"We double checked them for more caterpillars. They should be okay," Lexus said.

Ricky still checked the second leg in the jeans before he put them on.

"Lexus and I agreed that your legs would look a lot better with a little fur on them," Vincent said.

"Or if they were a nice shade of blue," Lexus said grinning.

"By the way, Vincent, once we get you to safety, what are your people going to think of us? I mean I hope your scientists won't want to take us somewhere and experiment on us," Ricky said.

"Maybe you," Vincent said. "Lexus is too beautiful to experiment on, and there's not enough of Bebo to make for a good experiment."

Ricky looked at Lexus and thought he saw her cheeks darken.

"I think you made her blush," Ricky said, happy for a chance to get the attention off himself.

"What's going on?" Bebo asked. He rubbed his eyes and sat up. He searched his pockets for any remaining flowers, but he had already eaten them all. "Do any of you all have any of my food left?"

"Here, Bebo," Lexus said. She handed him a few berries.

"Thank you," he said.

"I must be dreaming," Ricky said.

"What?" Vincent asked.

"Oh nothing," Ricky decided not to say that he was shocked that Bebo could actually say thank you.

The four marched on toward what they hoped would be the final obstacles to their destination. They walked slowly at first to allow Ricky's legs and feet to fully recover. By the time they reached the stream from which Vincent had gathered the water, Ricky felt a lot better. He considered suggesting that they stop so he could soak his legs in the water, but he knew they needed to keep moving. This planet might look like a paradise, but since they arrived they had encountered a lot of nasty creatures.

A flock of blue birds flew overhead.

"Reminds me of home," Lexus said.

"Don't tell me that even the animals are blue on your world?" Bebo asked.

"No, but the prettiest ones are," she said. She smiled, and for the first time Ricky realized that her teeth were a bright white. Not that he hadn't noticed it from the first time there was enough light to see her, but he hadn't thought about it. He tried to wonder how she would look with blue teeth.

"What are you thinking about?" Lexus asked. "Have I got a leaf caught in my teeth?"

"No. I was just thinking about how you would look with blue teeth."

"Blue teeth? Now that would look strange," Lexus said. "Would you want me to paint my teeth blue?"

"No, no, not at all. I just realized that while the rest of you is blue, your teeth are white," Ricky said.

"You haven't seen the rest of me," Lexus said with a straight face.

Ricky blushed, and Lexus laughed at him, but at the same time she took his hand in hers and held it.

"Actually people on my world do paint their teeth different colors to match their finger nail paint."

"In my world they paint their fingernails and toenails but--"

"Toenails?" Lexus interrupted. "We would never do that."

"You paint your teeth, but not your toes?" Ricky asked.

"Different worlds, different customs, I guess that's to be expected," she said.

"I think both your customs are strange," Bebo said. "We would never paint our body different colors. Why would anyone want to do that?"

"I guess to try to look more attractive," Ricky said.

"Or to be different," Lexus said.

"A lot of the people on this world will color their fur, especially the fur on their cheeks. It is usually done by the young adults when they are looking for a mate. I guess we do it for the same reasons you mentioned already."

"Vincent, do you have a mate, I mean someone special?" Lexus asked.

"I'm too young to have a mate, but there is someone who I hope will be mine when it is allowed," he said.

"Allowed?" Ricky asked.

"Yes, when we are between the ages of seventeen and twenty, our grandparents, parents, uncles, and aunts decide when we are ready. They do it by voting. If there's an even number, then the oldest relative gets a second vote."

"Wow, that's silly," Bebo said.

"Not really," Vincent said. "Once we are twenty we don't need their concurrence. Many get permission and yet don't marry for years."

"In our world only our parents decide who and when we can marry," Bebo said. "Doesn't that seem a more practical way of doing things?"

"Yuck," Lexus said. "My mom and dad haven't liked any of my boy friends."

Ricky didn't say anything since he hadn't had what he thought was a real girlfriend.

"They would just die if I brought you home with me," she whispered to Ricky.

"Why?" Ricky asked.

"Mainly because your blue coloring has faded away."

"In Florida, I think you could fit in, and I know my mom and dad would be crazy about you," Ricky said. Seeing the smile Lexus gave him for his remark, Ricky was glad he didn't say what he had thought, that he had seen a lot of strange looking people in Florida. He didn't say it because, despite thinking it about Florida, Lexus didn't look strange to him anymore.

They neared the thick forest and started hearing a variety of animal sounds. A distant roar stopped them all in their tracks.

"A torant?" Bebo asked.

"No, I don't think so," Vincent said.

"Whatever it was, do you really think it's safe to go in there?" Bebo asked.

"Would you rather have it see us out here in the open?" Ricky asked.

As if someone shouted "go," they all dashed for the cover of the trees.

"This is really thick. I don't think we should get too far away from each other," Lexus said.

"Yuck," Ricky said as he tried to remove a large leaf with thick sap that clung to his shoulder.

Bebo started to remove a similar leaf that he had stepped on. "Hey, this leaf might make a good shoe." Instead of pulling the leaf off his foot, he folded it over the sides of his feet and pressed it against the top of his foot. "The sticky stuff is only on one side of the leaf. Hand me that one, Vincent." Bebo pointed to a nearby leaf that had fallen from the tree.

Vincent picked it up and handed it to Bebo. Both handled the leaf carefully to avoid the sap. In a minute, Bebo had feet covered by the leaves.

"I hope the sap doesn't irritate your skin," Lexus said.

"It feels good," Bebo answered.

The screech of an animal echoed through the trees.

"I think that's just the walla. It's a large bird and it's harmless," Vincent said. "Let's go a little further in before we find a place to spend the night."

They walked another half hour. While they heard a variety

of animal sounds, they only saw a few birds and small squirrel-like creatures. They stopped for the night by a small lake. Vincent studied the water and the surroundings.

"I think it's safe to get into the water and to stay here tonight," he said when he finished his inspection. He cupped some water in his hands and took a sip. "Tastes good, too."

Bebo stepped into the water and stepped out. He looked at his new "shoes." The water didn't appear to affect them at all. Satisfied, he lay down in the water at the very edge of the lake. Only a few inches deep, the water didn't come close to covering him.

Ricky watched him and wondered what he was doing. He noticed that Vincent and Lexus were watching Bebo, too. They didn't have to watch long as Bebo started rolling back and forth in the water. After doing this a few time, Bebo got up and walked out of the lake.

"We need to start a fire. I'm cold," Bebo said.

Vincent located an open spot about twenty yards from the lake. All four gathered sticks, and Vincent used his pocket knife to light the fire. Like a Swiss Army knife, Vincent's small knife had a number of small tools built into it. Vincent snapped something on the knife that Ricky didn't have a good view of, but he did see the sparks that the pocket knife produced.

"Ricky, I would like clean myself in the lake, but I'd rather not be by myself. Would you come with me?" Lexus asked in a soft voice.

"Sure. Are you going to roll around in the water like Bebo?" Ricky whispered.

They both laughed.

They walked to the lake, and Lexus led them to a spot where

a few large boulders sat at the water's edge. "This will be fine," she said. She pulled off her sweater and placed it on one of the boulders. Underneath her sweater she wore a white undershirt that looked just like the ones his mother bought him from the JC Penny store.

Ricky stared at her a bit embarrassed and wondering if he should turn around to give her some privacy.

"Don't worry, that's all I'm taking off, other than my shoes."

"I, uh," Ricky started to say something, but he decided it might be best if he stayed quiet.

Lexus waded into the water until the water level reached her waist. She turned around to face Ricky and sat down. Only her head remained out of the water.

"You know it wouldn't hurt you to clean a little, too."

"Oh, yeah," Ricky said. He removed his socks, shirt, and shoes and waded in next to Lexus. "It's not as cold as I thought it would be."

"It feels good," Lexus said.

The two sat there under a bright moon and talked for a long time about lives on their respective plants. Finally, and a little reluctantly, they both got out of the water.

"It is cool once you get out, but I think I'll wait until I'm a little dryer before I put my sweater back on," Lexus said.

"Good idea," Ricky said and gathered his shirt and socks.

"Don't take this wrong, but you may want to wash that shirt and those socks before you put them back on."

Ricky looked at his clothes. His socks definitely needed washing.

"I don't mean to be rude," Lexus said.

"No, you're not. I do need to wash them." He placed them

in the water and rubbed them around in his hands until he thought most of the sweat and dirt were gone.

They found Vincent and Bebo asleep by the fire when they returned. They found a spot next to the fire and tried to get as comfortable as they could on the hard ground. Without any hesitation, Lexus snuggled in close to Ricky.

"If I haven't done so already, I want to thank you for saving my life today. I can't imagine falling into that grass and having the caterpillars crawl over my body. Thank you."

Ricky thought about what to say. He didn't even remember running the last twenty yards. He didn't feel like a hero. He wondered how to respond but fell asleep before he said anything.

Chapter 14

The buzzing of an insect around his face woke Ricky. He brushed his hand by his face and sat up. Bebo and Lexus were still asleep, but Vincent was gone. The sun had started its climb in the sky. The mountains in front of them prevented Ricky from seeing the sun, but the light from it had already brightened the sky above him.

Ricky stood up and walked to the lake. He saw Vincent standing about knee deep in the water and splashing water over the rest of his body. His clothes were stretched out on one of the large rocks near the one Lexus had placed her sweater the night before. They looked like they had been washed.

He hadn't seen Ricky approach the lake, and Ricky decided not to bother him. He walked back to their small campsite. The two were still sleeping, so he gathered some leaves that he thought he recognized for the group's breakfast. The vegetation they had eaten since their arrival wasn't bad, but he wished he could find a cheeseburger tree.

Lexus sat up when he arrived with the small stack of leaves.

"Good morning," she said. "If that's for all of us, thank you."

"It is. You two were still sleeping, and Vincent is down at the lake bathing."

"Is his whole body covered with fur?" she asked grinning.

"Yes, completely," Ricky said.

"When I get back home," Lexus laughed, "no one is going to believe any of this."

"Hey," Bebo mumbled, still half asleep, "is it time to get up?"

"Yes. I have breakfast," Ricky said.

Bebo sat up.

"Here," Ricky said. He leaned over and handed a couple of the leaves to Bebo.

"These are the good ones that we had the other day," Bebo said.

"I was wondering if we shouldn't wait for Vincent to make sure," Ricky said. He knew Bebo would likely go ahead and eat the leaves anyway, and he did.

"They're the same ones. I know my food."

"I imagine he does," Lexus said.

Vincent joined the group and confirmed Bebo's statement that they were the same leaves and good to eat.

"I think we'll get to the mountains before noon. Finding a way through them might take a while, but these mountains I'm familiar with because they constitute the border to this region."

"How about the sleeping gas?" Lexus asked.

"That area runs along the base of the mountains on the other side," Vincent said.

"How wide is the region with the gas?" Ricky asked.

"We think it's about a mile wide," Vincent said. "We have the far side marked with signs and a fence. The fence is only this high." He held his hand up even with his chest.

"Your people never tried to cross it with gas masks or other special equipment?" Ricky asked.

"Some have tried, but none ever returned. Most of those were seen collapsing shortly after entering."

"How do you know it's just a sleeping gas and not a poisonous gas?" Bebo asked.

"We've done an analysis on the gas. That's easy. We stuck a twenty foot pole into it with an instrument that could analyze the air."

"Makes sense," Lexus said.

"Additionally, some people have been overcome by the gas when they got too curious and a gust of wind blew some of it across the fence. More than one remained asleep for a full day before they either recovered or someone found them and took them away from the area. All of them were just fine when they came to."

"There's no way around it?" Bebo asked.

"No."

"One of us must be immune to the effects of the gas. That has to be the solution," Lexus said.

"I can't carry him across," Bebo said.

"No, but you could take a note across written and signed by Vincent explaining what happened. The note would request a wheeled cart in which you could push Vincent across," Lexus said.

"Excellent solution to a problem I had wondered about, too," Vincent said. "I didn't think anyone but Ricky might be able to carry me that far."

"What do we have to write on," Bebo asked.

"On white cloth, if nothing else," Lexus said. "We could use this to write with." She held out a small tube.

The three looked at it, but no one asked what it was. Ricky thought it looked like one of his mother's lipstick tubes, but didn't think Lexus carried lipstick with her.

They resumed their trek toward the mountains. A flock of dozens of red birds took flight as the group approached them.

"Do you smell that?" Ricky asked.

"Smells good," Bebo said.

"Smells like my mom is baking chocolate chip cookies," Ricky said.

"It's the orange flower. There are a lot of them over there," Vincent said and pointed to a cluster of plants. Other than the flowers, the plants looked like they might be dead. The thin branches had no leaves, just a flower or two on each branch. "I don't recommend eating them."

"Are you sure?" Bebo asked.

"They're extremely spicy. Some people eat them in contests and have suffered blisters in their mouth and throat."

The forest began to thin out. Ricky saw two animals that looked like deer in the distance. The animals saw him and ran off. He wondered what his mother and father were doing right now. No one would believe his mother when she claimed that Ricky had just vanished. He felt sorry for his parents. He wished there was some way he could give them a sign that he was okay.

He remembered the story about a boy who had vanished on his way home from school a year or two ago. The people on the news thought something terrible had happened to him, but what if he, too, had found a magic coin. Maybe he, like Ricky, had been transported to another world and was still there. What if he suffered the same fate and never returned? After thinking about it for a few seconds, it surprised him that he felt sorrier for his parents than for himself.

"Stop!" Bebo shouted. He had run ahead to a bush that had three large clumps of white berries.

The three looked to see what had startled Bebo into telling everyone to stop.

"Oh, Bebo, they're harmless," Vincent said. "We call them nuna. Some people keep them as pets."

It took a moment for Ricky to see the nuna. They were small animals that reminded him of the meerkats he had seen on television. It seemed like hundreds of them were running across the forest in front of them.

"Like a migration," he said.

"Aren't they cute," Lexus remarked.

In less than a minute, they were gone, and the four travelers moved on. They ate while they walked and talked about the animals on their home planets. The trees gradually gave way to open ground and the mountains. Unlike the mountains behind them and to their left, these did not have a solid face of rock that went straight up for thousands of feet. Narrow valleys separated individual mountains, and Ricky thought that the group might even be able to climb over them, if necessary.

"I guess one valley is as good as the next," Vincent said. "We might as well go that way." He pointed to the nearest valley.

"Okay," Ricky said, and the three followed Vincent's lead.

"Are you starting to believe we'll make it Vincent?" Ricky asked.

"I started thinking that some time ago. Although, I have to admit, I sometimes wonder if this isn't some sort of dream, and I'm still laying back there in the crash."

"Better the crash than the quicksand," Ricky said.

"If, I mean once we make it to safety, I'll make sure the three of you are amply rewarded," Vincent said.

"I don't think any of us want a reward. We just want to go home, and I don't know how we can make that happen."

"What kind of reward do you have in mind?" Bebo asked.

Vincent and Ricky grinned at each other.

"We could hold a feast in your honor Bebo. Since you come from a royal family, it would be the right thing to do."

Bebo smiled, "That would be so cool."

Lexus had not been paying much attention to the conversation. She seemed distracted by something in the mountain to their right.

"What do you see?" Ricky asked.

"Not sure," she answered. "Vincent, what kind of large animals live in your mountains?"

"Lots of animals, but what do you mean by large?"

"I thought I saw a very large animal watching us from that spot up there. I only saw its face, and at first I thought it was just a large rock, but then I thought I saw its eyes. After a few seconds, it backed into the mountain. I think there's a cave up there."

"There are always a lot of caves in our mountains. I guess it could be anything."

Ricky looked in the direction Lexus indicated, but didn't see anything. "As long as it stays away from us, I guess it doesn't matter what it was," he said.

"I hope so," Lexus said.

They entered the valley. At first, the valley was a couple hundred yards wide. After they hiked several hundred yards, the mountains started to squeeze in on them. Soon, they were walking on a narrow path with the ground on both sides of them sloping sharply upward. The path wound back and forth so much it was hard to tell what direction they were going.

They reached a spot on the trail where a large opening to a cave offered them a choice. The walls inside the cave contained ample light producing plants.

"What do you think?" Lexus asked the group.

"I don't want to go in there," Bebo said.

"Guess we should continue following this trail to see where it takes us," Ricky said.

The others agreed, and they decided to ignore the cave entrance. In another five minutes, however, the trail ended.

"We can either try to climb over the mountain or we can explore the inside of the cave," Ricky said.

"I think we should try the cave," Lexus said.

"I agree," Vincent said. "It's not uncommon for our mountains to have tunnels going through them. It may lead us to the other side."

"Only if we have light," Bebo said.

"Usually our caves either have light or they don't. That one seemed to have plenty of light, so I think we'll find light throughout the cave."

"Bebo, we can always take some light with us if necessary," Lexus said.

They walked back to the cave and entered it.

CHAPTER 15

"This is a large cavern," Vincent said. "Look how high the ceiling is."

"It's beautiful in here," Lexus said. "The light makes the walls look pink, and some of the larger crystals are a bright red."

"I'm just happy there's plenty of light in here," Bebo remarked.

"I think I hear water dripping somewhere," Vincent said. "If there's a stream we might be able to follow it out of the cave."

Ricky hadn't seen any stream coming out of the cave near the entrance they used, so he didn't know why it would lead them to an exit elsewhere, but he kept his doubts to himself.

Vincent started walking, and the three followed him.

Ricky noticed that the light producing plants grew everywhere, on the ground, walls, and even the ceiling of the cave. There was no one area where it was dark. Rather, there were pockets of the cave that were lighter or darker than others. It reminded him of the times when the power went off at home and his parents used candles for light. Here in the cave, it looked like someone had lit thousands of candles and placed them in different spots throughout the cave.

"Here it is," Vincent said. A small stream, barely a foot wide and an inch deep followed a depression that ran across the cave floor. Vincent put his finger into the water and tasted it. Without saying anything, he stood up and began following the stream deeper into the cave.

Bebo tasted the water and commented that it tasted good. He pulled a berry from his pocket and popped it into his mouth. "Slow down," he said to the others. They paused while he caught up. "You are always forgetting that my legs aren't as long as yours."

"And that you like to stop and eat more than us," Ricky said.

As they approached the end to the large cavern, Ricky studied the vast wall of the cave and did not see any tunnel or other opening that might allow them to go further. He thought that if he had said something earlier about his doubts, he could say "told you so."

"There," Vincent said.

At a spot where the cave wall appeared to overlap itself, Ricky saw what Vincent had discovered: a tunnel about four feet high and four feet wide. The small stream turned at a right angle at the cave wall and after traveling eight feet entered the tunnel. Vincent entered the tunnel without hesitating.

"Wait a minute," Bebo said. "How's the light in there?"

While Ricky ignored a lot of what Bebo said. In this case, he agreed with him.

"It's okay," Vincent said.

"Are we going to be able to find our way out if we start winding around in tunnels?" Ricky asked.

"We have caves and tunnels all over our planet," Vincent said. "We won't get lost."

"You must have a great deal more experience in them than we do," Lexus said.

"Enough to be careful," Vincent said. "We'll mark our way so we can find our way out."

"Okay," Ricky said. "Let's go."

Bebo grumbled to himself, but he kept up with the group. For a while both Ricky and Lexus had to walk bent over to keep from hitting their heads on the top of the tunnel. Just as Ricky's back started to hurt, the tunnel opened up into another large cavern. Before they moved away from the tunnel, Vincent marked the side of the tunnel entrance with an X, and Ricky stacked three flat rocks next to an interior wall.

"We can also tell this tunnel by the star shaped mark on the wall up there," Lexus said pointing to a spot about ten feet above the tunnel.

"Good," Ricky said. "This cavern looks bigger than the one we were in before."

"I'm not sure if we can even see the far end of the cavern," Lexus said.

"I vote that we turnaround," Bebo said.

"It seems silly for us to turn around without checking out this cavern. It's so big the far end may lead out of the mountain. Let's at least walk through the middle of it to the other end. The stream appears to run straight across. If we don't see a way out, we can return and go back the way we came," Vincent said.

"Come on, Bebo, I think we should keep going," Lexus said.

Bebo didn't say anything but gave his head a slight nod. The group started their trek through the large cavern.

"Why does the light look different up ahead?" Lexus asked.

"I think we may be in an old volcano," Vincent said. "Did you feel the temperature rise when we left the tunnel?"

"It is getting warmer," Ricky said. "You think that different shade of light is coming from the lava? I do smell something in the air."

"Maybe. We don't have any active volcanoes, but there are dozens that still simmer. This may be one of them, although I don't recall any being down in this region," Vincent said.

"Great," Bebo said. "If we don't get lost down here, we may get cooked."

"There's very little chance of an eruption while we're down here," Lexus said.

"Look over there," Ricky said after they had walked a little farther. A bright red glow lit up a small area behind two truck-sized rock formations that jutted out of the ground.

They moved cautiously toward the rocks and found a large pit in the floor of the cavern. At the bottom of the pit, they saw a river of red hot lava. It rolled slowly out an opening at one side of the pit and disappeared into an opening in the other side. Every second or two, a flame shot upward from the lava.

"There are more openings in the cave floor over there," Ricky said. It looked like every twenty or so yards, the ground had opened up in a number of spots above where the lava flowed.

"I suggest we don't walk anywhere on the ground above where we think the lava might be flowing" Vincent said.

"Let's get back to our stream," Bebo said. Ricky could hear a trembling in Bebo's voice.

"Good idea," Ricky said. He wiped sweat off his forehead. The hot air that rose out of the pit smelled terrible.

Shortly after they resumed walking on the side opposite the lava, the cave floor became littered with rocks of all sizes and the ground sloped upwards.

"Looks like there was a cave-in on this side of the cavern," Ricky said.

"You mean a landslide?" Lexus said.

"Yes, look at it. It looks like the wall collapsed and crumbled this way," Ricky said.

"That could have happened a hundred years ago," Lexus said.

"Or longer," Vincent said.

"I don't like this," Bebo said.

"I think we're safe here, Bebo, but first sign of trouble, we can turn around," Vincent said. "I don't want to put you at risk just for me."

"Tell that to the coins," Bebo said.

A loud shriek echoed through the cavern. Hundreds of birds or bats that the group had not noticed before took flight from various spots in the cavern. The shriek came again. It sounded closer.

"What was that?" Lexus asked.

"I don't know, but it sounds like it's coming from somewhere behind us," Vincent said.

"Looks like we won't be able to turn around, Bebo," Ricky said. "I think we might want to run."

No one needed more encouragement. The four sprinted along the edge of the stream and away from whatever had made that awful sound. They ran until the stream simply disappeared into the ground. They stopped, caught their breath, and listened for any sign that they were being followed. They couldn't see anything behind them, but they knew the creature could conceal himself in hundreds of places in the large cavern.

"I thought following the stream was a dumb idea," Bebo said.

"Hey," Lexus said, "it doesn't look like that thing followed us. It might not have any interest in us at all. Why don't we sit here for a second, drink some water, and finish these berries that I've been carrying."

Ricky didn't know if it was the thought of eating or Lexus' soft voice that got Bebo to relax. Bebo sat down and quit complaining. The four sat there and discussed their options. Ricky didn't want to turn around just to please Bebo, but he thought roaming around in this cavern would be more dangerous than trying to find a different valley that might take them through the mountains.

"I guess we should turn around. The stream gave us a good landmark to follow and not get lost. I still think we could explore a little longer, but maybe it's best to go back," Vincent said.

"Maybe not," Lexus said. "I think we should climb up the rock slide and find a place to hide. Now!"

She sprinted up the gradual slope of the cavern wall that had collapsed years before. The three boys followed her still unaware of what she knew or saw. Ricky took a peek back the way they had come and saw something that terrified him.

"What is that thing?" Ricky gasped while he ran.

"I'm not sure," Vincent said. "Luckily it's still pretty far away."

"Wait for me!" Bebo called from behind them.

"I'll get him. You two keep climbing," Ricky stopped and let Bebo catch up. Without any encouragement, Bebo leapt onto Ricky's back, and Ricky raced up the loose earth and rocks after his two friends.

In the few seconds it had taken for Bebo to reach him, Ricky looked at the beast that appeared to be chasing them. Initially, the creature reminded him of a dinosaur, a Tyrannosaurus Rex, but something was different about it. The word dragon didn't flash into his mind until he was already carrying Bebo. That's what it looked like more than a T Rex, but how could that be. At least dinosaurs lived at one time in the past, dragons were just imaginary creatures.

"A dragon," Bebo yelled. "It's a dragon. Run faster, faster!"

"Over there," Lexus shouted. She ran fast and was about fifteen yards ahead of them. Ricky had caught up with Vincent.

Behind them, the dragon shrieked. The loud, shrill noise sounded close and terrified them, but they kept running up the steepening slope. Ricky slowed to help pull Vincent over a pile of rocks, and Bebo jumped off his back and scrambled up to Lexus who had just disappeared into a small tunnel.

More shrieks echoed through the cavern.

"Hurry, Vincent," Ricky shouted as he tugged on Vincent's arm. "There are more coming, and I think they're flying."

The entrance to the dark tunnel was only a few steps away when a deafening shriek came from right above them. A shadow seemed to descend around them.

Chapter 16

Vincent and Ricky raced into the entrance of the tunnel. At least from the outside it looked like a tunnel. The entrance stood about six feet tall and four feet wide. The inside widened after just a few feet and extended for about another twenty feet, but then it came to an abrupt end. The tunnel was really just another small cave.

"I can't believe we made it," Ricky gasped. "That one was right on top of us."

"You only made it because the large one that swooped down from above first knocked the one chasing you on the ground away. I guess he didn't want to share."

A hissing sound at the entrance made them all back against the wall of the cave. A large grey head with bright purple eyes poked in through the entrance. A snake like tongue darted out between fang-like teeth. The dragon strained to get the rest of its body through the cave entrance.

"He's too big to get in here," Bebo said. Everyone relaxed a little, and Vincent sat on a large rock.

"I can't believe it," Vincent said. "They are supposed to be extinct."

"The dragons?" Lexus asked.

"Yes, I don't know when the last one was seen on our world."

"Well, obviously a few still exist," Ricky said. "How are we going to get out of here?"

The dragon withdrew its head from the cave.

"Maybe it will just go away, and we can continue our journey," Lexus said.

"I wonder why the first one we saw didn't fly. It appeared to run and even hopped as it chased us, but the other two or three I saw were flying."

"That's easy, Ricky, the one that was chasing on the ground had something wrong with one of its wings. It just hung limp on its side while it ran," Lexus said.

"I saw it, too," Bebo said.

Suddenly, one of the dragons scraped a foot against the side of the cave door. Small rocks and earth broke away. Realizing that it might be able to claw and dig its way into the cave, the dragon began to tear at the cave wall with fury.

"Oh, no," Lexus said.

"I don't think it will be very long before he'll tear down enough of the wall to get in here," Ricky said. He started studying the inside of the small cave looking for any exit. The lighting wasn't very good, but there didn't seem to be any way out. Then he saw it, a small opening directly above them, but was it too high.

"Look," he shouted.

"Put me up there," Bebo yelled.

Ricky lifted Bebo over his head. He strained to get Bebo high enough. Finally with Lexus and Vincent bracing him, Ricky was able to lift Bebo by his feet, and Bebo was able to reach into the hole and pull himself up.

"Lexus, you're next," Ricky said.

"No, Vincent should go next," she said. "You'll need my help to lift him up high enough."

"I don't know," Vincent said. "I prefer you go---"

"No," Lexus insisted, "you go now!"

Vincent didn't argue. Ricky didn't know what to say. He didn't want anything to happen to Lexus, but she did make sense.

"Here," Ricky said as he squatted. "Try to stand on my shoulders."

Vincent, with Lexus assistance, climbed up Ricky's back and stood on his shoulders. Ricky wasn't sure if he could stand up with Vincent's full weight on him.

"Let me help," Lexus said. She kept hold of one of Vincent's hands, and with her other hand she reached under Ricky's right arm. She lifted his arm as Ricky struggled to his feet.

Vincent's head and shoulders went right into the opening above them and with Bebo's help he climbed up and out of sight.

"How does it look up there?" Lexus asked.

"Does it matter?" Ricky asked her.

"I guess not," she said.

"It's a large area," Vincent said. "Lighting is not very good, but the air smells fresher. I think there's a way out."

The dragon at the entrance shrieked, and the loud noise vibrated in the small cave.

"How are you going to get up after me?" Lexus asked.

"I don't know, but you have to go. That monster is going to break through any minute now."

"You'll have to stack up some rocks. Make a small hill of rocks and maybe we can reach you and help you get up."

Ricky looked around and saw what Lexus was talking about. The cave floor was half covered with rocks, some as large as basketballs.

"Good idea!" he said. "Now get on me." He started to squat down.

"No, stay up. It'll be easier for you, and I can climb up."

Ricky remembered what a great climber she was, and sure enough, in a flash she had grabbed his shoulders and climbed up his back. To Ricky it felt like she took three steps and was standing on his shoulders. The next thing he knew she was gone. He looked up and saw her feet disappear through the hole above him.

He looked at the entrance and saw the dragon trying once again to force his way into the small cave. It looked to Ricky that the creature's hips were the only thing keeping it out. Ricky hurried from one rock to another gathering them into a pile directly below the opening. In just a few seconds, he had a pile at least three feet tall. He started to run to two other good sized rocks in the far corner of the cave when he heard the entrance to the cave start to crumble. He turned, ran back to the pile of rocks he had built, and jumped from it to the opening above him.

His out stretched right hand grasped the inch thick solid rock ledge, but his left hand brushed off the opposite side. His right hand started to slip when he saw Vincent's furry hand reach out and grab it. Ricky reached back up to the ledge with his left hand. A blue hand reached in and grabbed it from the other side of the opening. His two friends pulled him up enough that his head and shoulders were inside the opening.

The two struggled to get him higher.

"Vincent, let my arm go down to the ground. I can get myself through from here."

Vincent allowed Ricky's arm to move to the ground, but didn't let go. Once it was there Ricky used his arm to push himself a little higher into the opening.

"Now Lexus, you can let go."

As soon as she did, Ricky pushed his body up as high as he could. The opening grabbed at the back of his jeans, but Ricky was thin enough to make it through. He squirmed to get his legs through, and his two friends yanked him by his arms as a loud shriek shot up from below.

Something hit the toe of his right shoe, and then he was safe. Ricky thought he had snagged the shoe on a rock coming through the opening, but when he looked at it he saw that the tip of it had been bitten off. As soon as this realization hit him, the creature slammed its head hard against the small opening.

"Yikes!" Bebo shouted. "We better move away from here. The ground may cave in."

"I think this rock is pretty solid," Vincent said, "but it still may be wise to see if there is a way out of here.

"That thing almost got my toes," Ricky said. He sat on the ground and stared at his damaged shoe.

"Come on, Ricky, let's go see where this cave takes us," Lexus said. She took his hand and gave him a tug.

Ricky stood up. He felt a little dizzy but managed to walk alongside Lexus.

"We're going to be alright," she said and held onto his hand as they walked.

The few light producing plants provided barely enough light in the cave for them to see where they were going.

"I think we should walk toward the source of the fresh air," Vincent said.

"How can you tell where that is?" Bebo asked.

Ricky wondered the same thing. He thought the air felt fresher, but he had no idea which direction might lead them to its source.

"Can't you feel it?" Vincent asked.

"I can," Lexus said. "I think we're going in the right direction."

"Yeah, me too," Vincent said.

"We'll follow you," Ricky said.

"I wonder why the dragons didn't blow their fire breath on us," Bebo said.

"Fire breath?" Vincent asked.

"Yes. We don't have any dragons on our world, but one of our moons has all types of strange creatures, including fire breathing dragons. That's why none of us ever colonized that moon," Bebo said.

"You have moons you live on?" Ricky asked.

"Just one. The other one with all the dragons isn't safe."

"The dragons on our world are smaller and can't blow fire out of their mouths," Lexus said.

"I've never heard of the dragons on our world breathing fire, but I also thought they were extinct," Vincent said.

"On Earth, we have stories about fire breathing dragons, but I don't think they have ever lived there," Ricky said. "That one chasing us must have been fifteen feet tall. I guess it was a good thing it had a bad wing. If it could have flown, it would have easily caught us."

"I think it's getting lighter in here," Lexus said.

"It is," Ricky said. "There are more of those plants here, and I think we're getting close to the other side."

The four started walking quicker. Before long they could see a large opening to the outside and blue sky.

"I knew it," Lexus said. She put her arm around Vincent. "I knew we'd make it."

They ran the last fifty yards to the mouth of the cave but had to come to a sudden stop.

"Oh no," said Bebo.

They stood and looked out at the beautiful valley in front of them.

"How can we get down there?" Vincent asked.

They looked down at the ground a hundred feet straight below them.

"I might be able to climb down," Lexus said.

"It's a straight drop, Lexus," Ricky said. "Is there a way we can get over there?" He pointed to their right. Only about twenty feet away, a rock ledge at least four feet wide appeared to wind along the side of the cliff all the way to the ground below.

"How?" Vincent asked.

The four studied the cliff wall between them and the ledge. There didn't appear to be a single spot to hold onto.

"There's no way we can get over there," Bebo said.

"If we could get to one of those roots, they might be strong enough to let us swing across," Ricky said. Dozens of thick, long tree roots had grown out the side of the cliff wall and clung to it as they continued to grow down the side of the cliff. By leaning out, Ricky could see the branches of trees far above them.

"I don't think they're long enough to swing us across," Lexus said.

"I don't think they are either," Vincent said.

"Maybe we could just climb them. It looks like there's a small ledge above us," Ricky said. "I think it leads over to the other one over there."

"But we can't even get to the roots," Vincent said.

Ricky stepped further back into the cave and studied the rock wall.

"Bebo, come here," Ricky said. "Think you could get through that hole in the wall up there?" he pointed toward a small opening in the cave wall about four feet above his head. "If you look in it, you can see the sky."

"I don't know," Bebo said, "it looks pretty small. Besides, I can't get to it."

"You can if Lexus stands on my shoulders and you climb up on her," Ricky said.

"I can help support you," Vincent said to Ricky.

"It's worth a try," Lexus said. "You might see a way out for us."

"Okay, but I better not get stuck in there," Bebo said.

Ricky braced himself to support Lexus, and once again, she climbed up to his shoulders as easily if there was a staircase on his back. Vincent grabbed one of Ricky's arms to support his balance.

"You can make it through this, Bebo," Lexus said. She gripped the edges of the rock around the opening. "It's only a couple of feet to the other side."

Bebo climbed up Ricky and then Lexus.

"This is tight. I'm not sure if I can get through. Wait a

minute, okay, I'm out," Bebo shouted.

"What do you see?" Ricky yelled.

"I'm on a ledge, but it doesn't lead anywhere. I think if I climbed one of these vines I could get up to that other ledge."

"Are there any tree roots up there?" Ricky asked.

"A couple of long ones."

"Can you push the end of one of them over the entrance to the cave?" Ricky asked.

"Good idea," Vincent said.

"They're still attached to the ground in a lot of spots," Bebo said. "I can't break them loose."

"Bebo, come back to the hole," Vincent said. "Use this." He tossed his small knife up through the hole.

"Got it," Bebo shouted.

"Try not to damage the main root. Only cut the thin strands of the root that are attached to the ground," Ricky said.

In less than a minute, a vine looking root dangled in front of the cave entrance. Ricky reached out and pulled it to them. He tugged hard on it, and it felt sturdy.

"Let me go first," Lexus said.

Ricky didn't want her to, but he knew she was the lightest of the three and the best climber.

"Okay," Ricky said.

Lexus took the root and walked over to the side of the entrance. Gripping the root with her left hand she climbed up the side of the entrance to a point where she could wrap the root around her waist. In a flash she disappeared up the outside cliff.

Ricky and Vincent hurried to the entrance to watch her. They got to the edge in time to see her crawl to safety above them.

"Here it comes," Lexus shouted, and the root dropped down to them.

"You better go next," Vincent said. "I'm not as good of a climber as you are."

"Yes you are."

"No, and you're strong enough to pull me up while I climb. Please."

"Okay," Ricky said.

Ricky tried to copy how Lexus had climbed up the cliff, but quickly discovered the climb was harder than she made it look. He wasn't able to secure the root around his waist, so he held onto it in a tight grip which made using his hands almost useless in the climb. Luckily, the climb was very short, and he found three spots where he could place the toe of his shoe into small holes to help support him as he made his way up the six feet to safety.

He immediately threw the vine down to Vincent.

"I'm ready," Vincent yelled.

Ricky started walking backwards with the root and pulled as Vincent climbed. Bebo peered over the edge.

"You can do it! Only a few more feet," Bebo said.

Ricky saw Vincent's head appear above the ledge. Vincent squirmed up and over the ledge.

"Thanks," Vincent said and stood up. "What's Lexus doing?"

Ricky had been so busy helping Vincent that he hadn't checked on Lexus. He saw her clinging to the side of the cliff close to the ledge that led down to the prairie below. She appeared to be loosening the end of a large root so would hang freely against the rock wall. While he watched, Lexus finished her task and climbed back along the side of the cliff to them. As she returned she passed four other large roots that she had loosened enough to be used like rope supports.

"Okay," Lexus said. "We should all be able to get over to that ledge now. The cliff wall up here has several spots that you can grip with your hands or stand on. I loosened up those roots, so you can hang onto those as you go."

"Easy for you," Bebo said.

"I don't know," Vincent said.

"I think we can do it," Ricky said. He had his own doubts, but he knew it would be the only way to make it to the ground below them.

"Maybe if you carry me," Bebo said.

"Not this time Bebo," Ricky said.

"Bebo, trust me. It may look scary, but there are plenty of places to hold onto. We have you to thank for getting us this far. We would still be stuck in the cave below if you didn't crawl through the hole and toss the root down to us. I know you can do it," Lexus said. "I'll go first. You can watch and see how I do it."

Of course, Lexus made it look simple. Her feet seemed to have eyes of their own as they found one nook or crevice after another on her way across to the ledge. She barely used the roots for support, and Ricky wondered if she used them simply to show the rest how to do so.

"I guess I'll go next," Ricky said.

"I'll go with you," Bebo said.

"Just don't hang onto me," Ricky said. "I'll stop now and then and let you catch up, but don't grab me while I'm moving."

It turned out not to be a problem. They moved much slower than Lexus had, but in a few minutes, both stood safely on the wide ledge with Lexus.

"Your turn, Vincent," Lexus called.

Slowly, Vincent edged out onto the cliff and started moving toward them. He grabbed the first root as his foot slipped from a small rock that stuck out of the face of the cliff.

They all gasped, but Vincent was able to keep his grip on the root and regain his balance. He edged toward the next root but stopped a few feet short of it.

"I don't think I can make it!" he called out.

"Wait there!" Lexus shouted, and before Ricky knew what she intended to do, she was half way across the cliff wall to Vincent. She grabbed the root closest to Vincent and took it to him.

He took the root from her, and she guided him across to the next root. Before long, the four stood together on the ledge.

"Thank you," Vincent said to Lexus.

"You would have done the same for me," she said. "Why don't we finish this journey today? I think we have enough daylight to get across the patch of sleeping gas."

"I've been doing some thinking about that," Ricky said. "To be safe I suggest you walk ahead of us, Vincent. Since we can't see the gas, we won't know we're there until it starts affecting you."

"Sure," Vincent said. "That way you can stay near the edge of the gas field to see if it affects you."

"That's right. In case it does affect us all, I don't want everyone to pass out inside the area where the gas is strongest. If we stay right on the edge and experiment, I think we can hold our breath long enough to get each other back out if necessary."

"Good idea," Lexus said. "How much further do you think it is?"

They had walked a short distance from the mountain, and Vincent had told them the region of gas was next to the mountains.

"I don't really know. Like I said, no one has ever crossed it before. All I know is where it starts on the other side, and I think I can see the fence way out there already."

"So your people can see us approach it?" Bebo asked.

"Certainly, if any of them happen to be standing close to the fence and are looking this way, but that's not likely. Oh, I think….," Vincent collapsed to the ground before he finished his sentence.

"I think we're here," Lexus said. "Stay here, Ricky, Bebo, and I'll walk to him." She walked to him and kneeled down to look at him. "He's asleep, and I think our little buddy is too."

Ricky looked down and saw Bebo asleep on the ground next to him. He couldn't help but smile. "I'll take a few steps toward you, Lexus. If I pass out will you drag me back to safety?"

"Of course, but I think you're going to be fine."

She was right. He walked to them and even a few steps past but felt no effects from the gas.

"Looks like I get Vincent and you get Bebo," Ricky said.

He had to struggle to get Vincent up and over his shoulder, but with Lexus help he finally managed. Lexus joined him with Bebo thrown over her shoulder, and they started walking toward the fence.

"You know, I wouldn't be surprised if Bebo was faking just so someone would carry him for a while," Ricky said.

They both laughed and kept walking. Despite Vincent's doubts, a crowd of his people started gathering along the fence as they approached. They began to hear voices coming from the crowd and saw the looks in their faces.

"They don't sound too friendly," Ricky said.

"Yeah, I don't think we thought about this possibility," Lexus said.

Chapter 17

"Let's stop here for a minute," Ricky said.

The crowd that had gathered must have totaled twenty people by the time they stopped their approach. Ricky and Lexus stood fifteen feet from the fence. The crowd became silent when they heard Ricky speak.

"We're helping Vincent, your chosen leader, return safely to you," Ricky said. He couldn't remember Vincent's last name.

The people in the crowd stared wide-eyed at Ricky and Lexus.

"I know we look different to you, but we mean you no harm. Once Vincent awakens, he can explain everything to you," Lexus said.

An older looking person, his fur had turned mostly grey came to the front of the crowd.

"You say you have Vincent Wollitzer there?" he asked.

"Yes. His plane crashed back in there. We found him and have been traveling with him," Lexus said.

"Where are they from?" someone in the crowd asked.

"Why do they look so strange?" another asked.

"We can find that out later," the old man said. "Please bring Vincent out of the gas. We need him. There have already been some border clashes. We need to show the world he is alive."

"We will," Lexus said.

A funny looking vehicle with flags flying off its roof approached at a high speed. It seemed to be flying a couple of feet off the ground. From a distance, the vehicle looked like a big, green shoebox.

"The police," a voice in the crowd said.

"I need your word that we will not be harmed. We come as friends. Vincent will tell you when he awakens," Ricky said.

"We've already said that," Lexus said. "Come on, it will be fine."

They walked to the fence line.

The old man motioned to a couple next to him, and they reached out and took Vincent from Ricky. The two carried Vincent a few feet away from the fence and put him on the ground.

"Can you take Bebo?" Lexus asked.

"Sure," Ricky said. Carrying Vincent had tired him out. Ricky almost told Lexus he didn't have the strength, but he knew she had to be tired too.

"What or who is that?" the older man asked.

"He's our friend. His name is Bebo. The gas affected him, too," Lexus said.

"I guess you are not mullens," the old man said with a smile.

"What are mullens?" Ricky asked.

"Did Vincent not tell you? No, I guess not. It's what we call ourselves," he said.

"We call each other by our names and we're friends," Lexus said. "All of us were surprised at how each of us looked, but we accepted each other as we were. People who look different can still be friends."

"You are wise for one who looks so young," he said.

"Bring them over here!" The vehicle with the flags had come to a stop, and a heavyset individual wearing a blue vest over his clothing had stepped out of it. He began walking toward the group. He carried a cane that Ricky didn't think he needed for walking.

"I don't believe they pose any threat to us. They have saved Vincent Wollitzer. He is over there being tended to right now," the old man called back to him.

"Still, they will need to be examined, put them in the vehicle," the mullen who Ricky thought must be a policeman said.

"We wish to stay with Vincent until he has fully recovered from the gas," Lexus said.

"That will be up to him when he recovers, if he is really who you claim him to be, and if you have not harmed him," the policeman said.

"We have not harmed him," Ricky said. "How long does the effect from the gas last?"

"Not long, but my orders are to put you in the vehicle and to transport you immediately to the military base at Lupold," the policeman said.

Bebo groaned and moved. Ricky had all but forgotten he still carried Bebo.

"That ugly thing moved," the policeman nearly gasped.

"Let them first check on Vincent Wollitzer," the old man who had been kind to them said. "He's starting to wake up and is just over there."

"Are you an elder?" Lexus asked the old man.

"Yes, but I have little real authority," he whispered to Lexus. He turned back to look at the police officer.

"All right," snarled the policeman, "but make it fast."

"Did you know that our young friends had brought Vincent Wollitzer back to us when you responded to the calls from the citizens here?" the old man asked.

"No, just that some strange creatures were crossing the gas fields."

"Then I suggest you call your superiors and report his rescue. It is him. I recognize him from the photographs on the television."

The policeman walked back to his vehicle, and the old mullen turned to Lexus and Ricky.

"Let's go see, Vincent," the old man said.

"What's happening? Did the gas knock me out?" Bebo asked.

"Yes. We made it through. Lexus carried you all the way," Ricky said.

"Put me down. I can walk, I think," Bebo said. He staggered for a few steps before his balance came back to him. "What's going on?"

"We're not sure, but stay close," Ricky said.

Vincent was sitting up when they got to him.

"We made it," Vincent said.

"Yes we did," Lexus said. She kneeled next to him and took his hand in hers. "You are safe and have a world to lead, but I think we must leave you now."

"What do you mean? I want my world to get to know you and to thank you."

"I think we need to leave and go back to our own worlds now," she said.

The old mean leaned over close to Vincent. "Although there

is a lot I don't understand, Vincent Wollitzer," he said softly, "she is right. Orders have already been sent to take them into custody. There is great importance in getting you to the Temple as soon as possible, and you know how difficult it is to interfere with the internal affairs of a regional war lord."

"Maybe we should head back into the gas fields right now," Ricky said.

"I am truly sorry my friends. You saved my life and you safely returned me to my people. You should not be treated like this," Vincent said.

"We will be fine," Lexus said. "We have fulfilled the coin's purpose. I think now the coins will have a way for us to return to our own worlds."

"You have saved thousand if not millions of lives on this world," the old man said. "Armies of both nations have already started moving to the border regions."

"Then we must head at once to the Temple of Facall," Vincent said and stood up.

"Yes," Lexus said. "Goodbye, Vincent, I shall never forget you."

"I will never forget you all," Vincent said. He hugged all three of his new friends.

"Go save the world," Ricky said with a grin.

"I suggest the three of you leave now. Our policeman friend is heading back in this direction," the old man said.

Bebo leapt onto Ricky's back without any invitation. The three were back into the gas field and moving away from the crowd of mullens before the policeman reached Vincent. Ricky and Lexus looked back and waved. Vincent and the old man waved back. The rest of the mullens also started waving goodbye. The only one that didn't wave and didn't look very happy was the policeman.

"I imagine he'll take credit for Vincent's rescue in order to take some of the heat off of him for our escape," Ricky said.

"Aren't you happy?" Lexus asked.

"Yes, I am."

"Looks like even Bebo is smiling, too."

"Sleeping like a baby," Ricky said. "How do you think we get back home?"

"I don't know, but I'm sure it will be soon," Lexus said. "I wish you could come with me."

"I wish you could come to my home," Ricky said. "I bet my mom would love to meet you."

"You'd be the only guy around with a blue girlfriend," Lexus said.

"That's right," Ricky said with a laugh before what they had both said sunk in. He thought about it for a while.

Lexus stayed silent. She knew Ricky was considering what they both had said.

"I've never really had a girlfriend before," Ricky said. "I mean, I've never felt about any of them like I do you. I hope we both get to go home, but I know I'm going to miss you a lot."

"I'll miss you, too," she said and took hold of his hand. "We can't stay here. I just wish there were some way we could stay in touch. I wonder if the coins have future plans for us."

"I don't think it will be as frightening next time. I have to admit I was terrified when I first arrived here in the cave."

"We all were," Lexus said.

"What?" Bebo asked. He rubbed his eyes and shook his head trying to shake off the fatigue.

Ricky placed him on the ground. "I guess we're out of the gas."

"Seems so," Lexus said. "Which way should we go now?

"I don't want to go back the way we came. No dragons for me. Let's find a valley that will take us through to the other side, even if it takes forever," Bebo said.

"This time I agree with you," Ricky said.

They approached the mountain that they had come through and turned to their right, away from the ocean.

"It's going to be dark soon. It looks like that might be a way through the mountains over there." Ricky pointed toward a narrow valley that appeared to cut through two mountains. "I suggest we find a place to camp there for the night."

"I'm hungry," Bebo said. "Whether we can get through there or not, a couple of those bushes should make a good meal."

"You and your stomach, Bebo," Lexus said. "I'm surprised you aren't fatter."

"Fatter? I'm not even fat," Bebo said.

"Look at that fog," Ricky said.

A thick fog hung over the valley. It looked like a cloud that had somehow fallen out of the sky and got stuck between the two mountains. The sky up higher was clear in all directions.

"Maybe it's caused by steam seeping out of the mountain," Lexus said.

"Makes sense," Bebo agreed.

They walked into the valley and soon found a perfect campsite. It even had a small stream nearby.

"Look at the berries over there," Lexus said.

"Fantastic," Bebo said and dashed off toward the bush.

Lexus walked to the stream.

Ricky happened to look up and saw that the thick fog had dropped quite a bit. Now barely twenty feet above their heads, it drew closer by the second.

"Lexus, Bebo, look at the fog," Ricky shouted.

Lexus was busy washing her face and hands, and Bebo was focused on the berries. Neither appeared to have heard him.

Suddenly the thick fog surrounded them all. Ricky could barely see his outstretched hand.

"Lexus!" he shouted.

CHAPTER 18

"Can't see a thing out here!" Bebo shouted.

"Over here, Bebo," Ricky said somewhat calmer hearing Bebo's voice. He waited a second for Lexus to say something. Bebo, closer to him now, grumbled something about the fog. "I'm right here," he said to Bebo and to Lexus, if she could hear him.

All of a sudden, he felt strange. He thought he saw a hand reach out for him in the fog.

"Ricky," she said.

Ricky took the hand in his. He felt like he might get sick. The thick fog, was it poisonous? He bent over at the waist and closed his eyes.

The hand squeezed his. "Ricky, what's the matter? Are you all right?"

He recognized the voice and was surprised he didn't recognize it the first time. He looked up and saw his mother standing there, her hand in his. The sick feeling vanished. Somehow, he had returned to Disney World next to the small fountain.

"I'm sorry Ricky, but I just had to retrieve the coin for you after it went into the fountain." She took her hand from his. He saw the coin in her other hand. "I'm not even sure why I did it. Hope you're not mad at me, but as soon as that coin hit the water, I felt like I had to get it back for you.

She gave him the coin. He studied it closely, and for a second, he was sure the words "Thank You" appeared on the coin. They faded away as fast as they appeared.

"How long was I gone?" Ricky asked.

"Gone? Where? When?"

Was it all a dream? Ricky realized what his mother said, that only a few seconds had passed since he tossed the coin into the fountain. How could that be?

"Are you okay, Ricky?" his mother asked.

"Yes. At least I think so, Mom."

"Well, now that that's done, what should we do? We don't have that long before we have to meet your Aunt for lunch. Might as well get some excitement into our lives, don't you think?"

"Mom, would it be okay if we just went somewhere and got something to eat first?" He didn't feel like he wanted anymore excitement in his life.

His mother looked at him. Like all mothers, she could tell something was bothering her son. "Sure," she said.

They didn't have to walk far before they came to a small snack bar.

"What in the world happened to your shoe?" she asked while they waited in line to order. "They were almost brand new."

He looked down at his shoes. The toe of one of them was ripped off where the dragon had bitten into it. It did happen. It wasn't just some dream. He remembered Lexus and smiled. She must have gone home first. That's why she didn't answer his calls to her in the fog. She was the first to arrive on the planet, so it made since that she went home first.

"I'll tell you. I'll tell you the whole story, Mom. You won't believe me, and I won't blame you, but I have to tell someone."

"Of course, I'll believe you," she said.

They sat at a small table by the window.

"You saw these shoes this morning, Mom, remember?"

"Yes."

"I've been with you ever since. How could've I done this?"

She looked at him. She had already wondered the same thing.

"Just don't laugh at my story. I can't explain how it all happened other than saying the coin was really magical, but this is what happened after the coin hit the water." He paused for a second getting his thoughts together.

"Well, tell me," his mother said. Ricky could see she was interested.

He began his story.

THE END

THE MOUSE GATE SERIES

WHERE WILL THE GATE TAKE YOU NEXT?

Titles by Bob Doerr

Mystery Detective Suspense Thrillers

Dead Men Can Kill

Cold Winters Kill

Another Colorado Kill

Loose Ends Kill

No One Else To Kill

Caffeine Can Kill

-Greed Can Kill

Action Adventure Series

The Attack

The Group

The Assassins

For a complete list of books by Bob Doerr,
a previews of upcoming titles, a schedule of events
and more visit his website www.bobdoerr.com or
find him on Facebook.

A Mouse Gate Adventure Book
What's your adventure?
www.mousegate.com

Title: The Enchanted Coin

- Author: Bob Doerr
- Publisher: TotalRecall Publications, Inc.
- Paper Back: ISBN: 978-1-59095-084-5
- eBook: ISBN: 978-1-59095-085-2
- Audio ISBN: 978-1-59095-280-1
- Number of pages in the finished book: 130
- Publication Date: September 17, 2013

We have all heard of tales of UFO's, ghosts, people who say they can talk to the spirits, ancient curses, and magical talismans. Most of us automatically dismiss them as false, figments of people's imagination, and understandably so. However, might not just a few of them be true? I don't know, but I heard this story from a young man the other day who swore the fascinating tale I have set forth in this book really did really occur, because it happened to him.

You be the judge.

Title: *The Rescue of Vincent*

- Author: Bob Doerr
- Publisher: TotalRecall Publications, Inc.
- Paper Back: ISBN: 978-1-59095-279-5
- eBook: ISBN: 978-1-59095-280-1
- Audio ISBN: 978-1-59095-281-8
- Number of pages in the finished book: 130
- Publication Date: : October 28, 2015

Would you believe in the magic of a coin you discover that has your name inscribed on it? The coin claims to be magical and even has instructions for you to follow. Would you follow them? What if you did? Would you expect anything to happen?

That's what happened to Ricky Street. He found the coin and followed its instructions. What happened to him was totally unexpected and quite frightening. It led him to an adventure that many might think impossible to believe, but it did.

You be the judge.

Title: *The Magic of Vix*

- Author: Bob Doerr
- Publisher: TotalRecall Publications, Inc.
- Paper Back: ISBN: 978-1-59095-309-9
- eBook: ISBN: 978-1-59095-280-1
- Audio ISBN: 978-1-59095-281-8
- Number of pages in the finished book: 140
- Publication Date: August 4, 2015

Samantha Gillespie's discovery of a magic coin results in her transportation to the strange world of Vex where magic is real and where she has to overcome a number of challenges if she ever hopes to return home.

What happened to Samantha was totally unexpected and quite frightening. It led her to an adventure that many might think impossible to believe, but it did.

You be the judge.

For a complete list of books by Bob Doerr,
a preview of upcoming titles and more
visit his website www.bobdoerr.com or
find him on Facebook.

A Mouse Gate Adventure Book
What's your adventure?

www.mousegate.com